degrees OF GUILT

kyra's story
{DANDI DALEY MACKALL}

miranda's story
{MELODY CARLSON}

tyrone's story
{SIGMUND BROUWER}

{miranda's story}

{miranda's

story}

degrees of
Guilt

MELODY
CARLSON

Tyndale House Publishers, Inc.
Wheaton, Illinois

thirsty ™

Visit the exciting Degrees of Guilt Web site at www.degreesofguilt.com and Tyndale's thirsty(?) Web site at www.areUthirsty.com

Edited by Ramona Cramer Tucker

Designed by Julie Chen

Scripture quotations are taken from the *Holy Bible,* New Living Translation, copyright © 1996. Used by permission of Tyndale House Publishers, Inc., Wheaton, Illinois 60189. All rights reserved.

thirsty(?) is a trademark of Tyndale House Publishers, Inc.

Library of Congress Cataloging-in-Publication Data

Carlson, Melody.
    Miranda's story / Melody Carlson.
        p. cm. — (Degrees of guilt series)
Summary: High school senior Miranda Sanchez wants to change her boring life and, despite the concerns of her friend Sammy, she decides to become a "wild child," until her partying ends up in disaster.
    ISBN 0-8423-8283-6 (pbk.)
    [1. Conduct of life—Fiction. 2. Friendship—Fiction. 3. Death—Fiction. 4. Ecstasy (Drug)—Fiction. 5. High schools—Fiction. 6. Schools—Fiction.] I. Title. II. Series.
PZ7.C216637 Mi 2004
[Fic]—dc22   2003010302

Printed in the United States of America

07   06   05   04   03
7   6   5   4   3   2   1

Sammy James is dead. He died in my living room. Last night. Right there on the ugly purple sofa that Shelby hasn't even finished paying for yet. She'll freak when I tell her.

My hands are still shaking and I've thrown up four times, twice at home and twice at the police station. Mostly dry heaves after the first time, but it's like my body is trying to purge itself of the memory. When the police finally allow me back inside the apartment—after collecting all their "evidence"—I wander around from room to room like a zombie, trying to clean stuff up. But it's hopeless. This place will never be clean again.

Sammy, where are you?

I know I should rest, but I can't go to sleep. Or maybe I *am* asleep, and this is all just a hideous nightmare. I will wake up and everything will be back to what it used to be. I'll live differently, make better choices, and Sammy will still be alive. But I know I'm not asleep. The wail of last night's sirens still rings in my ears, and the flashing emergency lights are scorched into my brain like a sizzling brand that will burn there forever. But what's worse—and it makes me ache to remember—is how Sammy looked before they wheeled him away.

I never thought the first dead person I'd see would be one of my oldest and dearest friends. Or that I'd be the cause of his death. At first I thought he was just asleep. Okay, maybe passed out even. And that in itself didn't seem so surprising since I'd never seen Sammy drink anything more than a single beer in his entire life, and that was last New Year's, back when life was still normal. But even then I had been the one to talk him into it.

But for some reason Sammy really cut loose last night. At first I was pretty shocked that he even came over at all. I mean, Sammy has never been into partying in the first place. And even though the party was supposed to be a celebration—an "after the play" party—Sammy had still insisted he wasn't coming. If I hadn't given him that last back-stage hug after our final big scene—pressing myself fully against him—I'm sure he never would've come over here at all. Although I only saw him drink a couple of beers, he was definitely the life of the party for a short while. Totally un-Sammy-like. I was pretty wasted myself, but I can still remember thinking, *How weird is that?* But then, stupidly as it turned out, I said nothing, did nothing. Just kept on partying like I've done over the last few months.

Then Kyra shows up and finds her brother sacked out on the purple couch. She just totally loses it. "What's wrong with Sammy?" she shrieks.

"He's asleep," I tell her. "Wanna drink?"

"He is *not* asleep, Miranda!" she yells at me as she slaps him on the cheeks.

"Easy, girl," I say in what I think sounds like a soothing voice. "He just had a little too much to drink is all."

But she is shaking him now. "Something's wrong!"

Now I'm thinking she must be high herself and just flipping out. I mean, it wouldn't be the first time. "Hey . . . Kyra?" I put my hand on her shoulder. "Just chill."

"I don't need to chill!" She's screaming now, loud enough to be heard over the music, which is pretty cranked up. *"Call 911!"*

"Just a minute, Kyra." Now I'm getting seriously worried. Not about Sammy so much, because I'm pretty sure he's just passed out. But the kind of trouble I'll be in if the cops come in here and bust—

"Where's the phone?" she demands.

"Okay. I'll be right back." So I go to the kitchen, take the cordless phone off the hook, and drop it into the utensil drawer next to the stove. Then I return to the living room, where Kyra is shaking her brother's limp body. "Come on, Sammy. Wake up."

"Let's get him some coffee," I suggest.

"Just get him in the shower," offers someone else from behind me.

"Did you call? Where's the phone, Miranda?" Kyra leaps up and grabs me by the arm with an ironlike grip. "Call 911 *right now! I'm* not kidding!"

"Okay!" I yell as I pry myself out of her grasp and return to the kitchen. But I don't get the phone. Instead I stand like a dummy in front of the sink just wondering, *What should I do now? Do I call 911 and risk serious trouble? Or maybe I should get everyone out of here first, clean up the bottles and cans and—*

"*Miranda!*" Kyra's voice makes me jump. "Where is it? Where's the freaking phone?"

I look around the kitchen. "I dunno."

She takes off now, and I know she's going to Shelby's bedroom, the only other phone in our apartment—and not a cordless. I grab a garbage bag from under the sink and start heaving the empties into it.

"Party's over!" I yell toward the living room as I pour the remains of a vodka bottle down the sink, thinking it looks expensive and wondering if Mitchell Wade brought that.

"You guys help me clean up," I call out, but all I hear is the sound of music still pounding. I walk into the living room to see that everyone—except Dylan, Kyra, and Jamal—has cleared out. The others must've realized that Kyra was serious about calling 911. I pause now, garbage bag hanging limply from my hand, to look at Sammy. I mean *really* look. I drop the bag on the floor as I realize that Kyra is probably right. Something *does* seem to be wrong here. He is totally out of it. His face is so pale that his freckles stand out like chicken pox, and he is so still that I can barely tell if he's breathing. But I believe he is. I kneel beside him now and start speaking quietly into his right ear, because I know he doesn't hear very well from his left one.

"It'll be okay, Sammy," I promise as I push his hair from his damp forehead. So cold. I reach for the red chenille throw that Shelby doesn't like anyone to actually use. She says it's just for an "accent."

"Kyra's getting some help," I assure him as I tuck the soft blanket around him. His face looks even paler contrasted against the bloodred fabric. I can hear Kyra in the other room, her voice loud and tight—irritated, as if she thinks the person on the other end is an absolute moron.

I take his cold hand into mine and hold it to my flushed cheek, as if to warm it. "Hang in there, Sammy. Hang in there. It's going to be okay."

When the paramedics arrive, I'm still kneeling on the floor, leaning into the couch, and holding his hand against my face. I wonder how they got here so quickly, or if I blacked out for a few minutes. Even now I don't know for sure. But I hear Kyra's voice from below, screaming at them to hurry, telling them that it's just one more flight of stairs. And suddenly I am pulled away from Sammy and everything is happening fast. Too fast—like a blur. Voices and directions. I am pushed away, and a paramedic tears open Sammy's shirt as if he's not even a real person—as if he's a piece of machinery or one of those resuscitation dolls. And I hear snatches of phrases like "no blood pressure . . . cardiac arrest . . . possible overdose." And I think, *Overdose? Of what? A couple of beers?* I just don't get it.

Then the cops arrive. They usher me into the kitchen to ask me questions—too many questions. Not enough answers. I can't focus on their words. It's like every sentence is a Superball, just bouncing off one blank wall in my brain and smacking into another. I can't think straight—everything is ricocheting all around. I think I actually laugh when they start to recite my "Miranda rights." I'm thinking, *Did they make this stuff up just for me?* Then suddenly I sober up and want to know what's happening with Sammy. I jump up from the kitchen table and push past the policewoman and go into the living room and look.

They are carrying Sammy out on a stretcher. But I can see his face—can still see it now—just empty and blank, like a house with all the lights turned off. And somehow I know. I know it's too late. I know Sammy is gone. He's dead. And it's all my fault.

That's when I rush into the bathroom and throw up in the toilet. The policewoman stands in the doorway, watching, as if I'm a dangerous criminal, as if I might try to climb out the bathroom window to escape. She slowly shakes her head as she waits for me to finish and flush the toilet. I remember how I cleaned that toilet earlier today. Back when I was eager to impress Mitch with our little apartment, back when I thought I was, oh, something— so grown-up, so cool. I struggle to my feet and wash the vomit off my face with cold water. The coldness reminds me of Sammy—how cold he was— and I wonder. For the first time that evening I wonder if Sammy had something more than just a couple beers. And then I throw up all over again.

I'm going down, I think as I ride in the back
of the cop car to the police station. Miranda Maria
Sanchez is going down. And I don't even care. I
guess I know it's what I deserve. There's some satis-
faction in knowing this. Imagining myself behind
bars helps to take my mind off Sammy. I try not to
think about him.

Detective Sanders tells me to sit down in a row
of blue plastic chairs for a few minutes and wait for
her, but then I feel my stomach twisting, wrenching,
and I have to rush to the bathroom again. I throw
up–twice. Once again she is standing in the doorway, hands on her hips as she watches me. Is the
look on her face disgust? I wipe my mouth with a
rough paper towel and try not to see my image in
the fluorescent-lit mirror above the sink. I know I

look hideous. What would Mitch think of me now? What does it matter?

I hold my throbbing head in my hands as I sit in the chair in front of the detective's desk. It feels like my brain will explode if I let go. Maybe it wouldn't be such a bad thing, either. I can just see the newspaper headlines now—"Local Girl Dies of Exploding Head at Police Station." I hear the officer's voice but don't totally connect the words. I think she's asking about my parents. She has to repeat her question.

I look up at her and suddenly wonder what made her want to become a cop. She looks like a fairly normal lady to me—kind of middle-aged with short sandy hair, sort of like somebody's mom. I almost ask her about her career choice but then realize that's not why we're here.

"My mom's on a business trip," I finally say, relieved I actually came up with an answer.

"Do you know where she is?"

"She travels a lot. Sales, you know. I think she's in Atlanta this time." I surprise myself with my own coherency. "But I don't think she left a phone number." I don't mention Shelby's cell phone number. I'm not ready to talk to my mother just yet. What good would it do anyway?

"How about your dad? What's his name?"

"Julio." I sigh. "Julio Aldonzo Sanchez."

"But your mom's name is Shelby Bartlett, right?"

"Yeah. Shelby went back to her maiden name right after the divorce."

The detective's eyebrows lift. "You call your mom by her first name?"

I shrug. "It's what she likes. Makes her feel younger, you know. She pretends I'm her sister sometimes. Just around guys though."

She nods and continues writing. "So is your dad around?"

"He's kind of out of touch, if you know what I mean. He's stayed pretty much out of the picture during the last ten years—cheaper that way."

"You mean child support?"

"Yeah. Shelby puts pressure on him if he comes around. He doesn't like that."

"Any other relatives?"

"Just my grandmother—Helen Bartlett."

She looks back down at her notes. "Did I see a sign at your apartments—?"

"Yeah. It's Bartlett House. It was my grandfather's home when he was a boy. Then after he died, Nana had it remodeled into apartments, for the money, you know—not that it makes much anymore. The building's so old that most of the rent goes toward upkeep anyway, and the two units below us aren't even rented right now. My mom wants to sell the place when I graduate." I'm thinking I should say *if I graduate.* Somehow it seems unlikely right now.

"I thought you said it was your grandma's place?"

"Yeah, but my mom's gotten legal guardianship . . . uh, Nana's not doing so well these days."

"What's wrong?"

"Alzheimer's. She's in a nursing home."

The detective nods. "Too bad."

Yeah, I'm thinking, *too bad. Too bad for me.*
Maybe I wouldn't be in all this trouble if Nana was
still around.

"Do you have a family lawyer?" she asks. "Or
someone you'd like to call?"

"Don't you have to be rich to have a lawyer?"
I ask.

"Or in trouble."

"Like me?"

Just then the phone rings. The detective picks
it up and says, "Uh-huh. Too bad." She frowns as
she makes a note of something. "Uh-huh. Yeah . . .
interesting." Makes another note. "I'll get back to
you on that one."

I watch her closely. I suspect, based on her
expression and glance toward me, that it's about
Sammy. I feel like I can't breathe. Maybe I'll sit here
and suffocate. Just fold over and collapse on the
dirty linoleum floor. "Local Girl Dies of Asphyxia-
tion at Police Station."

She shakes her head. "Your friend didn't make it,
Miranda."

I close my eyes and feel my front teeth bite into
my lower lip. Hard. I taste the blood—salty warm.
And I just sit there, saying nothing. I can't believe
this is really happening. Maybe it's not. Maybe if
I wait long enough, I'll open my eyes and be someplace else, like Mitch's English class. Daydreaming
again. My favorite one—about how he and I will
run away together shortly after I graduate. We'll
drive away in his silver Porsche, and everything
will be fine.

Then I hear someone clearing a throat, and I glance up. It's Detective Sanders. She's still here. I am still at the police station. This is not going to go away.

"Samuel James died, Miranda. They believe it was cardiac arrest." She writes something down on the paper in front of her, then looks up at me. "Strange that a healthy young man of 17 should have a cardiac arrest. Don't you think?"

I nod.

"Now you say that all you kids were doing was alcohol, right?"

I nod again. "Just beer and wine." Then I remembered the bottle of vodka. "And, well, I did notice a bottle of vodka too. You know how these things go—" I studied her neat uniform and "perfect look" hair. "Don't you?"

"What *things?*"

"Parties. You know, everybody brings a little something to share. A six-pack of beer, a bottle of wine. You know, whatever they have on hand."

"Or whatever they can get their hands on. Or get some *grown-up* to buy for them at the local convenience store. Or sneak from their parents' liquor cabinets. Oh yeah, I know."

I stare down at my lap. For the first time since I've gotten into this whole partying thing I actually feel ashamed. Before, I always felt it was pretty cool and kind of risky to sit around drinking and talking with my friends, acting like we were all grown-up and so sophisticated. Now the whole thing makes me feel plain ignorant. Stupid, even. As I sit here in

the glaring light of the police station, I feel ashamed.
For the first time since Nana's diagnosis I am truly
thankful that she'll probably never get wind of
this—or if she does she will simply forget about it
by suppertime. Alzheimer's has its perks, I guess.
Then I imagine Shelby reading the headlines as she
flies home: "Macon Teen Incarcerated on Murder
Charges." I wonder what she will think.

"But it does seem odd, doesn't it?" the detective
continues, bringing me back to the bigger reality
here. "Strange that your friend would drink a couple
beers, then suffer a cardiac arrest? Not your typical
reaction to a little alcohol."

Sammy. She keeps bringing us back to Sammy.
But it's as if a part of my mind wants to forget this
incident. Like if I can just block it out, then maybe
it'll disappear completely. Like it never happened.
But I can tell by her fixed expression that this won't
be possible. She's not going to quit questioning me
until I give her some real answers—information. I
take a deep breath and try to remember that business
about my Miranda rights. Miranda has rights? Okay,
I know I have the right to remain silent, to have a
lawyer. But what does it matter, really? I know I'm
already in big trouble. Going down. Why not just
spill my guts and get it over with?

"You already know I was drinking," I tell her.
"So my memory isn't as clear as normal, you know."

"I understand that, Miranda. I just want you to
tell the truth. Do your best, okay?"

"Okay. Let me think a minute, see if I can get
things straight."

She moves over to her computer, then keyboards something in. As she waits, her face is illuminated into this sickly shade of purple, coming, I'm sure, from the blue screen in front of her. But even so it creeps me out. It makes me think of a TV show where they always show the people in the morgue. And I wonder, *Is that where Sammy is right now?*

She pushes her chair back and peers at me. "You don't have any priors, Miranda. So far all we've charged you with is an MIP—minor in possession of alcohol."

"Are you going to put me in jail?"

She sighs. "Not likely. We just want a complete statement from you—something to help us make sense of Samuel's death. Are you willing to cooperate?"

"I'm willing to try."

She opens a drawer and pulls out a tape recorder. "Do you mind if I use this?"

I study the small black instrument and wonder if I'm being a total fool right now. I wonder what Shelby would say about all this. I can just see her stomping in here in one of her designer rip-off suits and stamping one of her high-heeled pumps, insisting that I handled this whole thing all wrong. But, hey, what's new about that? And what do I care about what she thinks anymore?

Still, I've seen enough law shows on TV to know that I should probably insist upon having a lawyer present. But what kind of a lawyer would I get anyway? Some low-life, court-appointed dude who can't get a real job? And even if I had the best legal

defense available—what was the name of O.J.'s attorney?—how could that change anything anyway? It
sure won't change what I did—the choices I made.
And it won't bring Sammy back.

So why not just get it over with? Why not just
tell what happened? Simply speak the truth into
this innocent-looking recorder and then take the
consequences. I can remember Nana telling me,
more than once, that the truth will set me free.
Pretty words, yeah, but I'm afraid that Nana and
her Bible are both wrong this time. If anything,
the truth could get me locked up for good. But isn't
that what I truly deserve? Wouldn't Sammy still be
alive right now if it wasn't for me?

Oh, Sammy, where are you?

While Detective Sanders goes to get us both a cup of coffee, I struggle to remember how this whole nightmare first started. How did I go from Miranda Sanchez, honor student, good athlete, and editor of the school paper, to Miranda Sanchez, party girl now wanted for the murder of her friend? To figure out this mystery I think I must go back a ways . . . but how far? I try to remember. Perhaps it was New Year's Eve, just a few months ago. I think that's about the time that everything—including me—began to change. . . .

■   ■   ■

"Miranda, you're still in your sweats," Shelby chirped that night as she paraded past me in her latest "party" dress, a bright-colored number with sequins that looked like they'd be falling off before the clock struck twelve.

"Yeah?" I examined her fire-engine red, spike-heeled, strappy sandals and wondered how this strange blonde chick could possibly be my mother.

"Well, aren't you going out tonight?" She puckered her glossy lips into a pouting expression. "It's your senior year, Miranda. You should be *out* there, having a good time. Have some fun, *girlfriend.*"

I'm sure I must've rolled my eyes at her. *"Fun?"*

"Yeah, go on a date—or out with some friends—isn't there a party going on *somewhere* tonight?"

Well, that just made me furious. "Shelby, you're a real piece of work. I mean, how can you even think about partying on the same day you took Nana to that smelly old nursing home?"

She laughed. "Oh, is that your big problem? My poor stuffy Miranda. Don't you know that Nana doesn't even know where she is anymore?"

"That's not true. She actually cried when she noticed we were leaving. I saw the tears in her eyes!"

"That woman cries when she can't find her peanut butter."

"But she's your mother—"

Then Shelby got that look—the one that means "Don't mess with me, missy." She actually used to say that to me when I was still shorter than her. But that night she just put her hands on her hips and stuck her chin out as she glared up at me. "Don't you dare go laying some heavy guilt trip on me tonight, Miranda Maria. It's your stupid choice if you want to sit around here and mope, but I've got places to go and people to see. Get it? And you are not, I repeat *not,* going to bring me down. *Comprendé?*"

Her limited use of Spanish was always meant to be a slam—a way to put me right in my place. It used to hurt a lot more, back when I was younger. I still vividly remember the day she came by school to pick me up early, and no one believed she was really my mother. She thought it was funny—like everyone thought she was too young and pretty to have a kid in second grade. Not to mention a Latina kid with serious eyes and a mop of wild black curls.

Of course I knew, even back then, that she had gotten pregnant with me when she was only 17—a whole year younger than I am right now. Too weird. But I think it was around then that I first took real notice of the differences between her and me. Naturally she would point these out to me during the years to follow. She was always quick to mention my big feet. Hers are a diminutive size six. Mine are an 11. And my big teeth. She used to call them my "horsey teeth," like it was some big joke. Fortunately I grew into them. My feet, well, that's a different story. But it didn't hurt that, despite both my parents' small stature, I eventually grew to be five-foot-eleven—an asset in sports, but not so much where dating is concerned. My dad told me once, back before he left, that I took after his father, who had been quite tall for a Mexican. Shelby said that's an oxymoron—a tall Mexican. But that's my mom for you. I happen to think I take after Nana. She's only five-foot-eight, but that was considered fairly tall for her generation.

But back to New Year's Eve. I spent the whole night basically moping around and feeling sorry for myself. I knew that Kyra had gone to a party with Tyrone Larson, which seemed pretty out of the blue, at least to me. And I know I could've gone myself— she even offered to set me up with Tyrone's buddy, Hale Ramsey. Ha! Now I don't like to judge people, especially since I know how it feels, but Hale is, well, kind of a hayseed. I mean, sometimes he seems pretty cool, and other times he's just a total hick. I wasn't sure if Kyra was trying to help me or make me look like the village idiot. Anyway, I declined. I told her that I still felt bad about breaking up with Jamie Cantrell.

"Get over it, Miranda," she'd told me on the phone.

"But he's really a nice guy. And he told Sammy that I broke his heart."

"He was beneath you. You need to move on. Destroy and conquer."

I laughed. "Yeah, that sounds real pretty." Some-times I think Kyra has no conscience when it comes to guys. I'd never say this to her face, but her use 'em-and-lose-'em attitude bugs me. Sometimes I think if she was a guy, I would absolutely hate her. And yet she's almost like a sister to me. We've been friends since grade school. And even when I went through my big-feet, buck-teeth stage, she was kind to me. Okay, this was only when no one else was looking. But who could blame her? She was this pretty blonde cheerleader, witty, smart, loved and admired by everyone. And I was, well, a geek. There was even a period of time—I think it was in eighth grade—when it felt like Sammy was my only true friend. And that was pretty inconvenient sometimes—like when I needed to borrow a tampon or something.

So on New Year's Eve I went to bed mad—at precisely ten-thirty—and woke up mad the next morning. Sure, I was still upset about Shelby's total lack of concern for Nana. But on top of that she'd brought some lame excuse for a guy home with her. I'd heard them come in around three. I could tell by his voice that he was new—someone I'd never met. But what really irked me was how Shelby and I had already discussed this particular problem before, and she'd sworn to me that she wouldn't do it again.

I woke up that morning and went into the kitchen only to discover this slightly balding, potbellied guy guzzling right out of the orange juice carton, wearing nothing but his stupid Joe Boxer boxer shorts with a small rip in the seat. Give me a break! Well, in a complete fury I walked right out of the apartment, down the stairs, past Nana's old and vacant apartment, and right over to Kyra's house.

I hadn't even taken a shower and still had on my sweats from the night before, but fortunately I'd had the good sense to grab a heavy coat on my way out. It was freezing cold outside. Several inches of snow had fallen during the night. But I was so enraged that I don't think I actually noticed the cold until I was about a block from the James house. I remember being a little embarrassed as I knocked on the door. It was pretty early, especially for New Year's Day. When Sammy, the consummate early riser, opened the door, even he looked as if he'd just crawled out of bed.

"Happy New Year," he said with a crooked smile.

"Yeah, whatever."

"Well, aren't you a little Merry Sunshine today." He held the door open wide for me to come in.

"Tell me about it."

Seeing the concern in his eyes now, I knew I had to be careful. Sammy knows me so well that it's scary sometimes. He can read me like a book. "So what're you doing out this early, Randi?" He'd been calling me Randi since fifth grade, back when I used to beat him playing one-on-one basketball games in front of his house. Back before he finally got his height.

"Just out for my morning constitutional, you know." I forced a goofy smile.

"On New Year's morning?"

I rolled my eyes at him. "Yeah, sure. Where's Kyra anyway?"

"Probably in bed." He grinned. "She pulled a late one last night."

"I figured." I started to push past him toward the stairs.

"I thought maybe you'd been with her . . ."

I turned around. Despite my foul mood I had to smile as I studied him standing there in his white T-shirt and flannel bottoms with—I'm not kidding—yellow ducks on them. He looked so sweet and goofy with his brown hair sticking out in tufts and his chin in need of a shave. I actually reached over and felt the bristles. "Looks like you lost your razor, bud."

"You don't look so hot yourself. Everything okay?"

I sighed. "Yeah, just dandy. I need to talk to Kyra."

"Well, watch out. She might chew your head off for waking her up. She sounded pretty mad last night. I think her date with the Ty-man went south on her."

I considered the possibility of vexing Kyra this early in the morning. I mean, this is one girl you don't really want to have mad at you. And after all, we'd only become good friends again just this year. I stuck my thumbnail in my mouth and started to bite what little was left there as I thought about my options. It was quite likely I'd taken too much for granted by showing up here this morning. On the other hand, I needed a friend. I paused and looked at Sammy.

His brows lifted slightly. "But you can talk to me."

And so I followed Sammy into his kitchen, a beautiful work of art that his mother had recently gotten remodeled to make their already perfect home even more so. I pulled out a wrought-iron stool, sat down at the granite breakfast bar, and watched as Sammy attempted to make a pot of coffee. Judging by the blackness of the brew, I suspected he was still fairly new at this. And, completely oblivious that Sammy was a guy—a guy who has more than once claimed to be in love with me, but always followed by a quick joke—I poured out my troubles. I drank three cups of his strong coffee and talked and talked. And he listened. Sammy was always the best listener.

Oh, Sammy, where are you?

Later on that morning, Kyra came out to discover Sammy and me shooting hoops in their driveway. It had been Sammy's idea. First we'd shoveled the snow. He thought it would be a nice New Year's surprise for his dad. Even after knowing Sammy all those years, it continued to amaze me how he was always thinking about others. Anyway, Kyra looked clearly distressed. One hand was draped dramatically across her forehead, and a deep frown shadowed her face. "Do you guys have to make so much racket down here? Every time that stinking ball hits the backboard it feels like it's slamming right through my brain."

"Too much partying last night?" I asked nonchalantly as I winked at Sammy.

"Too much something. You were smart not to go,

Miranda." She leaned against the rail fence that lines their driveway and groaned.

"How did it go with Tyrone?" I ventured as I set up my shot from the left, shot, and missed.

"Don't ask."

"Told you he was a jerk," said Sammy as he grabbed the rebound and dribbled for the basket.

I started to guard him, then stopped and turned my attention back to Kyra. "So we're both having a great New Year's Day, huh?"

"Oh, sure, you're done with me now." Sammy walked over with the ball under his arm. "Just like that, you dump me for my sister."

I rubbed my finger across his bristly chin again. "Hey, you need to go clean up anyway."

He laughed. "You should talk."

"Yeah." Kyra made a face at me. "You look like—"

"Believe me, I can imagine. But it's been a tough morning, you know. Don't kick me while I'm down, okay?"

"Fine. What do you want to do today anyway?"

Really, I just wanted to talk, to tell her the part that I couldn't bring myself to tell Sammy. But I could tell that Kyra was hoping for something a little more interesting, original, and fun.

"D.J. and Jamal are supposed to be over at the Den for lunch," offered Sammy. "I told 'em I might drop by later." He smirked at me. *After* I clean up."

"Wanna go grab a bite, Miranda?" Kyra shoved her hands into her pockets and waited for my response. As usual, she looked great—typical Kyra style. And I could tell her jacket was new, probably a Christmas gift from her aunt in Minneapolis, the one who always picked out the coolest stuff. Not for the first time, I wondered why I didn't have an aunt like that.

"Sure," I finally agreed. "I probably need to eat something to tame this coffee buzz I got going. What'd you put in that brew anyway, Sammy?"

"Secret formula." He waved as he walked toward the house. "Guaranteed to get you bouncing off the walls in no time flat."

Kyra shook her head. "Great, not only do you look like a bag lady, but you're going to be all hyped-up too. This should be fun."

Unfortunately, Kyra's car was in the shop. And so, looking like the odd couple, we decided to brave the elements and actually walk toward Macon's illustrious downtown. After just one block, it started to snow again. I shook the flakes from my tangled mop of hair and wondered why Kyra even put up with me.

"I've decided to reinvent myself," I suddenly announced as we shuffled through several inches of accumulated snow.

She laughed. "I thought you already did that when you quit working for the school paper and dumped that geek, Jamie."

I frowned. "Jamie's not a geek. Not really. Just ask Sammy."

"Yeah, yeah—that's a little like the pot calling the kettle black. But what do you mean, Miranda? What kind of reinventing are you talking about? You don't need any implants, that's for sure. And your hair's just great." She glanced at me. "Of course, a shower and some personal hygiene wouldn't hurt."

I shook my head. "I'm not talking about appearances exactly. But who knows? Maybe that'll change too. I'm talking about attitude. I need to get some attitude."

"Now you're talking, girl. You go get you some attitude."

"I've decided I'm sick of being goody-goody Miranda. I mean, how many girls do you know whose moms are having more fun than them?"

"Shelby hang one on again last night?"

I sighed. "Actually she came home with this total loser. But that's beside the point. I've decided that I'm going to change. Going to lighten up. Have more fun. You know?"

"Good for you. It's about time."

"Yeah, it hit me last night that this is my final year in high school, and my life is one great big yawn. Totally Boresville. I even went to bed at ten-thirty! On New Year's Eve! What on earth is wrong with me?"

Kyra laughed. "Nothing we can't fix."

"All right. Are you with me?"

"You bet. I've been waiting a long time for you to finally wake up and—"

"Smell the coffee!" I exclaimed as we reached the door of the Tiger Den. "From now on I'm doing whatever makes me feel good. It's not like Shelby gives a rip about my life anyway. And Nana, well . . ."

Kyra turned and eyed me. "Oh, I forgot about that. How's she doing?"

"I don't know, really. We just took her in yesterday. I'll stop by and see her tomorrow. Not that she'll know me. Last time she saw me she thought I was the milkman. And we don't even have a milkman."

Then we were inside the Den, and all seriousness was checked at the door. As usual the place was hot and stuffy and smelled like old grease and stale coffee. D.J. and Jamal were already there, and Kyra slipped right into their booth like they'd personally invited her.

"Sammy said you guys were here," she said lightly, her eyes zeroing in on D.J. Not that I blame her, since D.J. is pretty easy to look at, even though he can be a jerk at times. "Sammy said he'll drop by later."

I sat down and forced a smile to my face. But as we joked and bantered with these jocks, I suspected why Kyra had been so anxious to hop on down to this greasy little spoon. She had her sights set on D.J. now. Well, that poor boy wouldn't have a chance. To say that D.J.'s not the sharpest crayon in the box might be a bit of an understatement. But still I had to wonder what someone like Kyra could possibly see in him. Of course, she'd already dated almost every guy in school—so, why not?

Then something totally weird happened. It was right out of the twilight zone. We were sitting there in the booth just minding our own business and playing our little game of "which Macon citizen looks like which famous celebrity?" when this guy walked in. Not any ordinary guy, mind you. I swear this guy, unlike your average Macon citizen, really *did* look like a celebrity. Kind of a young Harrison Ford, only way more so. And he was dressed like someone you'd see in Manhattan, not that I've ever been there. But he also had a suntan, like someone who'd spent a lot of time on a beach. And this was January! Well, obviously, I couldn't take my eyes off him. And he actually looked our way. Not glanced either—I mean he *really* looked. Now I seriously doubt that he even saw me. Good grief, I looked like something the dog had dragged in with my grimy slept-in sweats and wild-woman hair. But I'm pretty sure he was looking at Kyra. And I know for a fact that she was definitely looking at him.

So I suppose that's the day when everything started to change for me. In fact, I'm sure of it. Oh, I didn't fully understand it at the time. That day in the Den I figured this handsome stranger-dude was just passing through our little hole-in-the-wall town. We all watched him leave too. Practically pressed our noses against the window like toddlers. Well, maybe not Kyra. She's too cool to do something like that. But we all stared in this sort of awed silence as this absolutely gorgeous man climbed into this equally gorgeous car. Some kind of Porsche, D.J. said. But it was silver and sleek and totally unsuitable for an Iowa winter. That's what made me so certain he was only passing through.

But of course, I was wrong.

The following day I went to Oak Haven to visit Nana. I found her sitting in the "dayroom," although I have no idea why they call it that. Do they also have a "night room"? She was fully dressed, with buttons done right and polyester pants pulled on correctly, and was sitting contentedly by the window. For a moment, I thought she was better. She looked so normal. So much like the Nana I'd known while growing up.

"Hi, Nana," I said to her as I moved a chair across from her.

As she turned, I thought I saw a glimmer of recognition in her eye. Then she asked, "Are you Clara?"

Clara was Nana's older sister. She died a few years ago, but the last time I saw her, she was rather plump with short white hair. So I didn't quite see the resemblance. "No." I spoke plainly. "I'm Miranda, your granddaughter."

She shook her head. "That's impossible. I don't have a granddaughter."

And so I decided to pretend that I was just a stranger and proceeded to talk to her as if we'd only just met. This was a trick I'd learned about six months ago, a couple of years after Nana had been diagnosed with early-stage Alzheimer's. That's when she first began forgetting important things, like people's names and where the bathroom was located. Up until then we'd simply assumed she was having a few memory lapses. Shelby used to say she was getting senile, although it seemed a little early at sixty.

"I'm a senior in high school," I told her.

"That's nice. Are you a candy striper? Are you going to bring me my lunch?"

I glanced at my watch to see it was nearly four. "I think you've had your lunch already, Nana."

"No." She firmly shook her head. "I would know if I'd eaten lunch. And why do you call me Nana? That's a silly name. My name is . . . Harriet. No, that's not right. Beulah?"

"Helen?" I tried.

"No, that's not it. It's Harriet. No, I mean Harry. Yes, that's it. My name is Harry."

I smiled. "Okay, Harry. Anyway, this is my last year of high school, and I'm thinking it's time to have some fun. What do you think, uh, Harry?"

"I think that sounds nice. Do you like chocolate?"

"I do. How about you?"

"Yes, I believe I do."

"Next time I'll bring you some," I promised.

"Yes. Make sure that it's that purple kind."

"Purple." As if that made sense. Tears were building in my eyes, but I tried not to let her see. Not that she'd care or even notice. Her concerns seemed to focus entirely on herself and her strange little world. Nothing like the Nana I'd grown up with—the friendly woman who'd be waiting for me to come home from school and tell her about my day. This was someone else.

The old Nana had been caring and considerate. Totally unlike her daughter. The old Nana had always kept her Bible close at hand, and she was fond of telling me things like "God loves you and has big plans for your life." She'd always clung to the deep-down conviction that God wanted to be involved with us on a daily and personal basis. She acted as if she carried on actual conversations with him. Like he listened every time she spoke. Now that I think about it, she might've been getting delusional then. But at least she was happy, and she always remembered my name and how to make oatmeal cookies that could melt in your mouth.

Finally, I could think of nothing more to say to her, and it seemed she was getting bored with me. She kept looking over my shoulder as if she expected someone really interesting to show up. So I told her I had to go.

"But you'll come back?" Suddenly she peered up at me like she really cared.

I told her I would and that next time I'd bring her

some chocolate. But I was also sure that by then she'd have forgotten that she'd even asked for any.

By the time I got back to the apartment, Shelby had already gone out, hopefully not with that obnoxious Joe Boxer man again. Anyway, feeling discouraged about my lackluster little life—especially after my exciting New Year's resolution—I called Kyra. But it was Sammy who answered and promptly informed me that she'd gone out with D.J.

"Oh yeah. I forgot about that."

"How's it going?"

I knew he probably meant the stuff I'd dumped on him yesterday morning. And now I kind of regretted spilling my guts like that. "Okay, I guess. Shelby acted like she was all sorry for bringing home that stupid guy. She promised it wouldn't happen again." I forced a laugh. "I'm not holding my breath."

"So what're you up to tonight?"

"That's where I was hoping Kyra would fit in. I really felt like doing something fun tonight. Especially since this is our last Saturday of Christmas break."

"Yeah, me too."

"But *I* want to do something totally different, Sammy. I mean, I wanna do something crazy, wacky, wild."

"Like what?"

"Oh, I don't know. I just figured Kyra would think of something."

"I'm sure she would too." But I could hear the

question in his voice, like he was wondering what was up with me. "Hey, you wanna do something crazy with me, Randi?"

I laughed. "Yeah, sure, Sammy. No offense, but you're not exactly the crazy type."

"And you are?"

"I am now."

"Now?"

"Yeah. It's my New Year's resolution. I just wanna go crazy and have some fun. Hey, maybe you should think about trying it yourself."

"So what've you done so far?"

I thought about that and sighed. "Well, nothing really."

Now he laughed. "Well, how about if we both get crazy tonight?"

"You serious?"

"If you are."

"You're on."

"I'll be there in five minutes."

"Okay." I hung up the phone and then, without even thinking, went to the fridge and pulled out four cans of Shelby's beer. I seriously doubted that she'd notice . . . or even care, for that matter. She'd probably assume that one of her beer-guzzling buddies had consumed them—maybe even Joe Boxer. I knew she would never in a million years suspect her straight-laced daughter had made off with them. I got out my big green parka and stuck the cans into my pockets, then went downstairs to wait for Sammy.

I saw his old red pickup just turning the corner, going a little too fast considering the icy streets.

Okay, I was thinking, *maybe old Sammy is ready for crazy.* I hopped into the truck and grinned. "This is gonna be fun."

"What should we do?"

"Something exciting."

To start with, Sammy drove over to the BigMart parking lot and cut cookies and spun out and swirled around until we were both laughing pretty hard. Then, when he stopped for a breather, I pulled out a can of beer. "You want?"

His eyes widened as I removed my gloves and popped the tab. "Uh, you know, Randi, besides not being of legal age, there's an open container law in our state. You probably shouldn't drink that in my truck."

I nodded, then took a swig, trying to conceal the fact that I think beer tastes like cold tea that's been brewed with dirty socks. "I know about the law. That's what makes this crazy, huh?"

"Maybe we should get out and walk around," he suggested.

"Works for me." I climbed out and took another big swig, almost choking to get the foamy bubbles down. But I was determined. Then, as Sammy came around to my side, I reached into another pocket and pulled out a shiny can. "Come on, Sammy," I urged. "You said you'd get crazy with me tonight. You're not gonna make me drink alone, are you, buddy?"

He studied the can in my hand and then finally took it from me, popped the tab, and took a long swig—almost as if he'd done it before. But I really didn't think he had. We started walking now, congenially swigging our beers and strolling toward Hunter's Glen, the subdivision that threw a hissy fit when BigMart decided to locate their shopping complex so close by.

"That's Coach Reynolds' house over there." Sammy pointed to an uninteresting newer home across the street.

"Uh-huh." I paused to look at it, leaning against a fire hydrant. "I'm quitting basketball, you know," I told him.

"Why?"

"Because it doesn't fit in with my *fun* plans. Besides, Coach Ashwood is too tough on us. She takes everything way too seriously."

"That's 'cause you guys are good." Sammy pointed across the street. "You should hear Reynolds ragging at us about how you girls could whip us if you wanted."

I laughed. "Yeah, sure. You guys are pretty good too."

As Sammy took another swig, I realized my beer can was empty now. Feeling like a magician, I pulled another one out. "Presto!" I said proudly.

"How many you got in there?"

I grinned. "As many as it takes."

It's amazing how you can make yourself like— or at least tolerate—something, if you're really determined. It seemed like no time at all before my second can of beer was empty. And suddenly, perhaps because it was my first time to drink more than just a sip or because I hadn't eaten dinner, I could really feel a buzz coming on. My arms and legs started getting loose, as if someone had oiled my hinges. And then I suppose I started to act pretty silly. I think I even flirted with Sammy. I can't remember whose idea it was to build a snowman on Coach Reynolds' lawn, but it seemed like a great plan at the time. We worked so hard to roll those big balls, and Sammy kept having to shush me when I got giggly. Luckily it didn't appear that anyone was home. When our creation was finished, I put on the finishing touches—three beer can "buttons" right down the front of the snowman's big round midsection. "It's a beer belly!" I told Sammy, laughing at what I thought was a pretty funny joke.

Sammy wanted to take the cans off, but I wouldn't let him. I imagined the local newspaper coming out to take a photo, then featuring it on the human-interest page. "Inebriated Snowman Mysteriously Appears in Coach's Yard."

Then, as we started heading back to the truck, I pulled out the fourth can of beer. "You want?" I asked in a slightly sloshy voice.

"No, thanks, I'm the designated driver."

"You betcha." I popped the tab.

Sammy peered at me. "You sure you wanna drink that, Randi?"

"Guess it's up to me to keep the crazy coming." Before we reached the pickup I'd downed my third beer and was feeling pretty loopy. I'm not really sure about the things I said, but I think I was really coming on to Sammy about then. And, as I recall, he wasn't stopping me either.

Finally, as we were standing out by his pickup

in the vacant BigMart parking lot, I threw my arms around his neck and soundly kissed him, right on the lips. I do remember *that*. I gave him one big sloppy kiss. To my surprise he kissed me back. And in a flash of an instant, I was sobered. By what? I'm not even sure. But I pulled my arms away and stepped back. I told him that I should probably get home, that I wasn't feeling so great. And I wasn't. I actually thought I was about to barf. Not from kissing Sammy. No . . . but because all that beer was just swirling around in my otherwise empty stomach, making me queasy.

I never did throw up that night. Instead I crashed and slept until about 2 A.M. That's when I woke up from a sound sleep with what tasted like a dead horse in my mouth, and I wondered what on earth I had done. Had I totally ruined my friendship with Sammy? I mean, he was one of my best friends. He had been there for me since grade school. Friends like that just don't come along every day. To throw that away was worse than crazy—it was insane!

But I was pretty wasted. So, instead of beating myself up even more, I decided not to think about it just then. And, I reminded myself, my resolution was to have fun and get crazy. Pushing thoughts of Sammy aside, I got up and made myself a tuna sandwich and sat in front of MTV until I finally fell asleep again.

The next afternoon, Sammy called. I tried to act nonchalant, or maybe amnesiac, like nothing out of the ordinary had happened the previous evening.

"I just wanted to let you know that I didn't think anything of it," he said.

"Of what?" I continued my dumb act, thinking Kyra would be proud of me—for my acting skills, that is, not for lying to her brother.

"Oh, you know. I don't want you to think that I'm assuming we are going out now or anything, Randi. I realize we're still just friends."

"Of course." Relief washed over me. "And I always want to be friends with you, Sammy. You've been the best friend to me."

"Yeah. I know. You too. But can I tell you something? As a friend, I mean?"

"Sure. Go for it."

"Well, I kind of understand why you're doing it."

"Doing it?"

"You know, your little resolution."

"Oh yeah."

"But I just think you should be, well, kind of careful, Randi. Sometimes I don't think you realize that you're this totally cool girl. And you've got so much going for you with sports and stuff. I've seen kids really mess up when they start drinking and partying and stuff. Like some of the guys Kyra's hanging with lately. I sometimes actually worry that she's not going to make it home some night—"

"Aw, come on, Sammy. It's not like Kyra or I are into anything dangerous. Just a little fun, you know? I thought you were having fun last night too."

"I was, kind of. But at the same time . . ."

"Oh, it's okay, Sammy. I know you've got your high standards and your dedication to sports and church and stuff. And that's cool. I can deal with that. But if you're really my friend, you gotta let me be me. And I'm thinking the same goes for Kyra too. You're a good guy, Sammy—the best. But you can't live our lives for us."

"I know. I just wanted to say something—as a friend, you know."

"Yeah. I appreciate it."

"Okay, then."

And so we said good-bye. In that simple phone conversation there seemed to be a breaking apart—like he was going his way and I was going mine. I remember feeling slightly sad when I hung up, but I wasn't even sure why.

Oh, Sammy, where are you?

They say your life flashes before you in the seconds that precede your death. Although how anyone would really, truly know this is highly questionable. But I wonder if that's what happened to Sammy tonight. I know it's happening to me now, as I sit in the police station, talking with the detective. Okay, maybe not my entire life. But a lot of the more recent things come flying at me like jet-propelled puzzle pieces. I'm not sure where they all fit or what they mean. Maybe I'll have time to examine these things more closely once they lock me up. I feel fairly certain they will now. And why not?

So far I have confessed to hosting the stupid play party, encouraging Sammy to come, even though I knew he was not into partying, enticing him to drink a couple of beers, and then—here's where they should throw away the key—refusing to call 911 when Kyra showed up and realized Sammy was in real distress. Sounds pretty incriminating if you ask me. Worthy of manslaughter charges at the least.

I take a sip of my now-cold black coffee that tastes like a mixture of metal, mud, and plastic, and I ask the detective to repeat her question. "Sorry," I mumble. "I guess I'm not focusing too well right now."

"It's understandable," Detective Sanders says. "It's pretty late. And I'd let you go home, Miranda, but sometimes it's better to get a statement while everything is still fresh in your mind." She looks down at her notes. "I asked you about an adult male, a Mitchell Wade, who was reportedly at the party."

I sit up straighter in my chair. "Who told you that?"

"The D.A. who's been assigned this case."

"A D.A.? What do you need a D.A. for?"

"Miranda." She says my name slowly as if I'm a five-year-old. "Did you hear me earlier? We all think it's a little strange that your friend would have a cardiac arrest as a result of having two beers. Don't you agree?"

"I don't know. Maybe there was something wrong with Sammy's heart. Maybe it was, you know, congenital or something."

"There's that possibility," the detective says slowly. "The autopsy will reveal that in time, and we should have the lab work for his blood content by tomorrow. But you seem like an intelligent young woman to me. Don't you think it's somewhat likely that Samuel overdosed on some sort of illegal drug substance?"

"No way! Sammy never, and I mean *never,* did drugs. Not even weed. He wasn't a partyer or drinker or anything. Last night was really an exception for him and, really, that was just a couple beers, and only because I pushed him. Honestly, you can ask anyone. Sammy didn't do drugs. He wouldn't."

"Well, time will tell." She sighs as she writes something down. "How about the other kids at the party? Were any of them doing drugs?"

I don't answer.

"Look, Miranda, if you're going to cooperate, then just cooperate. If you're going to keep protecting your friends, then let's take you home."

"I already told you that it doesn't seem right to tell you their names."

"And what if one of them has something to do with Samuel's death? Would it be right then? Or should that person be free to walk the streets?"

I press my hands to my throbbing temples. "I don't know."

"Okay, let's go back to this Wade fellow. I already know that he's an adult and that he's a teacher at your school. I have an eyewitness who says this guy was at your party. A witness who thinks that Mitchell Wade might somehow be partially responsible for Samuel's death."

I wish she would quit calling him "Samuel." He never liked it.

"Miranda—" she leans forward—"was Mitchell Wade a guest at your party?"

I bite the edge of my thumbnail and consider my answer. Just the fact that Mitch is an adult who was present at a drinking party with minors is probably going to get him into some serious trouble, not to mention fired. How can I rat on him?

Of course he was there. Without Mitch it wouldn't have been much of a party. I mean, he just walks into a room and everything springs to life. Conversation becomes exciting, sparkling—"scintil-lating" even, as Mitch would say. He's just like that. Besides, we were celebrating our big night. Mitch had done a brilliant job of directing us in *As You Like It,* a play by William Shakespeare. How could he not have been there? Mitch Wade was the main reason I'd wanted to host the party in the first place.

I still remember the first time Mitch actually noticed me. Vividly. It was the first day back at school after Christmas break. There we are, sitting in first-period English, when the same gorgeous stranger who had ordered coffee at the Tiger Den walked in. As it turned out, he'd been hired to replace old Mrs. Overstreet for the remainder of the year. Talk about an upgrade. Well, even our cool, calm, and normally collected Kyra almost fell out of her chair when this hottie walked in and very suavely introduced himself as Mitchell Wade, our new English teacher. Then he played this little game where he tossed a baseball to each of us and we told him what our New Year's resolutions were before we tossed it back to him. Kyra was at her best that day, shooting out this complete barrage of witty comments, to get his attention I'm sure. I also think it may have been a camouflage to conceal her indignation, since it took him forever to toss the ball her way. And yet I knew how she felt. It's like he was avoiding both of us. Or perhaps, as I imagined at the time, saving the best for last.

Anyway, I will never forget the feeling in the pit of my stomach when he finally tossed the ball to me. This electric sizzle came right through the smooth leather of the baseball, still warm where his hands had just touched it. I felt his eyes boring into me, as if he could see right into my soul. As if he liked what he saw. I'm sure it was then and there I was totally smitten. Such a stupid expression, but I think it adequately describes what happened. Of course I didn't let on about this to anyone else. How stupid would that be? I saw the other girls literally swooning over him, and I knew I did *not* want to look like them. But it wasn't easy. Even Kyra couldn't hide her interest.

But I remember what I said as my eyes locked with his. Without missing a beat I said, "My resolution is to lighten up and have some fun for the remainder of my senior year." I balanced the ball in the palm of my right hand, holding it at shoulder height. "No more Goody Two-shoes." This brought a ripple of laughter from the room. Then, without blinking, I pelted it back to him. "And what's yours, Mitch?" I asked, surprising even myself.

He smiled. "To make myself completely at home in Macon."

Well, welcome home, I was thinking. Then I got a little worried as I wondered if this almost unearthly man might possibly be able to read my mind. That's when I noticed Sammy looking my way with a sad expression on his face. As if he thought I had become totally hopeless, like my life was on its way right down the toilet about then. And maybe it was. But, oh, what a flush!

Within the first couple of days, I knew I had Mitch's full attention. Of course, I'm sure that's what a lot of us girls were thinking. I know Kyra was. But maybe we were all wrong. *Maybe it was Mitch who had all our attention.* Because every time he spoke to me, I felt as if he and I were the only ones in the room. And when he bent over my desk to show me something in a book or a paper, he always rubbed his shoulder just lightly against mine, and I could smell his cologne—Calvin Klein, Obsession—and sometimes even feel the warmth of his breath, a mix of pipe tobacco and something like licorice. Sometimes I thought I was going to melt into a puddle right there in the middle of the classroom. A great big Miranda puddle.

On Friday of that first week, Mitch asked me to talk to him after class about a paper I'd written about letting go of our inhibitions. I knew I was a good writer, since I'd been working on school newspapers since sixth grade. It's one of the few things I feel confident about. And I'd sweated bullets over this particular essay. I really wanted to wow him.

"This is technically well written," he said as we

stood by his desk. He handed me my essay, his hand brushing against mine, lingering ever so slightly. He smiled as he looked into my eyes. "But something's missing, Miranda."

I looked down at my paper, then back at him with a confusing mixture of hope and disappointment. "What's wrong with it?"

He put his hand on my shoulder. Not in an entirely unteacherly way, but just the same, it was something more too. "Not wrong, Miranda. Just not quite there yet."

I frowned. "But what—how do I get it there?"

He patted my back now. "Now *that's* the spirit. You've got to dig deeper, push harder. You're only scratching the surface here. I have a book that I'd like you to read. Have you ever heard of Jung?"

"Isn't he a philosopher or something?"

"A psychiatrist, but also a philosopher. One of the greatest. Read some of his writings and see what you think. But don't worry if you don't understand it all. No one really does. Just find whatever it is that really pushes you. Focus on the words that make you uncomfortable, the thoughts that compel you to think more deeply. And then let's talk about it."

"Really? You have time for that?"

He laughed. "Of course. It's not like Macon is abuzz with activity these days. So drop by my bike shop if you like. I'm there most of the time. Bring me a cup of joe and we can discuss Jung."

I smiled. "I'd like that." I hesitated, trying to decide how to say this. "You know, I was thinking about joining you on your bike workouts—maybe in the afternoons. I quit basketball, and already it feels like I'm getting out of shape."

He slowly shook his head. "No way, Miranda, you are definitely not out of shape. But I'd love to have you join us just the same."

"Okay, then. I guess I will. I just hope I can keep up with you."

He winked. "I have a feeling you'll do just fine."

The first time I biked with Mitch I wore my regular sweats, but he teased me and said I'd never be a biker without the right gear. So I withdrew some money from my college savings, an account I've been adding to since grade school, and got an expensive pair of black Lycra biking pants and a slim-fitting turquoise top that Mitch thought would look good with my hair. I must admit I did look pretty hot in my new biking outfit—like "watch out for the curves" kind of hot.

But here's what really got my attention—in the past I'd always tried to conceal the contours of my body. I'm not exactly sure why, except that back in middle school I started to "blossom" before any of my peers, and I know I felt pretty self-conscious as a result. But somehow—I'm sure it was due to the open admiration of a guy like Mitch—I suddenly began to feel much more comfortable with my body. Even my big feet didn't seem so terrible anymore. Mitch said they were "long and slender" when he fitted me with biking shoes. And he also said I had the "build of a Greek goddess" and that I could probably get a job as a professional model if I wanted. Man, did he know

how to feed my ego. And like a starving orphan,
I ate it up!

Kyra wasn't too thrilled when she heard that I
was biking with Mitch four times a week. I asked
her to join us, but she declined. "Sorry, Miranda,"
she told me, peering at me as if I were a couple cards
short of a full deck. "But I'm just not into freezing
my face off in the middle of winter. I'll think about
it again when the weather gets warmer." But even
though the weather has warmed up, I'm fairly positive that's not going to happen now.

To my surprise, Detective Sanders keeps her word and finally allows me to go home. "I think I've pushed you hard enough for now, Miranda," she says as she drives down my street. "But please give my questions some more thought, and hopefully you'll be willing to give us more answers on Monday. By then we should know the real cause of Samuel's death."

She pulls up in front of the apartments. "Yeah, I'll think about it," I say as I climb out of the car.

"You okay?" she asks, leaning across the passenger seat to peer up at my face.

I frown at her. *"Okay?* One of my best friends died in my living room last night. I doubt I'll ever be okay again."

"Do you still have that card I gave you?"

I nod. "But I'm not sure I want to talk to this guy."

"He's just a counselor, Miranda. Anything you tell him will be completely confidential. He can help you work through this whole thing."

"I'll think about it." But even as I walk away I know I won't. The last time I went to see a counselor was shortly after my parents split up. The guy kept asking me if I felt like I was to blame. And I honestly didn't feel like I was the reason for their breakup. If anything, I was the reason they'd stayed together. The reason they broke up was because Shelby had a boyfriend at work. It was no secret either. And according to Shelby, although I still don't know if this is true, my dad had had several girlfriends over the years as well. "What's good for the goose is good for the gander," she'd told me lightly, like that should explain it all. But this counselor dude kept going down the it's-not-really-your-fault trail, which can get pretty irritating to an eight-year-old, and finally I just quit going to see him altogether.

The ironic thing is that I really believe this whole situation *is* my fault. I know that if I hadn't pestered, actually enticed, Sammy to join in our "fun," he'd be alive right now. Maybe I should go see that other counselor dude again, and this time I could tell him he'd been right all along. For as it turns out, everything really *is* my fault.

I finish picking things up, washing things down, carrying the trash bags—evidence of the party— downstairs to the trash bin. Fortunately Shelby rarely takes out the trash so I'm not too concerned about her seeing all the empties piled down there. Not that she won't hear about the whole thing anyway. Detective Sanders assured me of this. I figure if I break the news first it might be easier. But what am I supposed to say? "Hey, Shelby, just thought I'd mention that Sammy James died on your purple sofa last night. See ya round." And then duck out the door. I don't think so.

I go to my room and look at my bed. It's no longer neatly made like it was yesterday, before the big party. Obviously someone—probably a pair of someones—decided to make themselves at home in here last night. The patchwork quilt that Nana made is all twisted and pushed against the wall. The pale green sheets, clean yesterday, are now wrinkled and have crumbs of food as well as a stain of something spilt—probably beer, since I already picked up several empties from in here. I rip the sheets from the bed and heave them into a pile by the door, then spread out the quilt, as if to hide the nakedness of the bare mattress. I lie down on it and long for sleep. If only I could escape this nightmare for a while. But I've already tried. It's just not happening for me.

I wish I were a little girl again, small enough to climb into Nana's lap and have her hold me and gently stroke my hair as she assures me, "Everything will be okay. God is watching over you." But Nana's locked up in the loony bin, and I am way too big for her lap. As I lie on my back, staring up at the constellation that's still adhered to my ceiling, the kind that glows in the dark, I wonder why it is I haven't actually cried yet. But I feel no tears coming. Just this terrible weight that sits on my chest like a huge stone, a crushing boulder that's steadily squeezing the life and the breath right out of me. I'm thinking the sooner it happens the better. I exhale all my air and wait for the world to go black.

But the phone's sharp ring jars me from my impending stupor, and I go to Shelby's room to answer it. Glancing around once more to make sure everything is back in its proper place—since this room was also utilized during the party last night— I pick up the phone and say hello. But my voice sounds dead. Flat and toneless, as if it belongs to someone else.

"*Miranda?*"

I know his voice, and there is a small speck of comfort to hear it. But uneasiness also washes over me. I'm not even sure why. "Mitch?"

"I heard the news. It's so unbelievable. Are you okay?"

I shake my head in answer.

"Miranda?"

"No," I mutter. "I am not okay. I will never be okay again."

"Poor thing. I wish I could come over and help you through this. But you know how that would look."

"I know."

"Did the police question you?"

"Yeah, I was there all night. They didn't bring

me home until just a couple hours ago. I haven't even slept."

"Poor Miranda."

"I feel so awful, Mitch. So responsible and guilty and horrible. I don't know what to do."

"Did you say anything to the police?"

"Yeah, I told them it was all my fault. I told them they should go ahead and lock me up. That Sammy would be alive if it weren't for me."

"You told them all that?"

"Yes. I figured my life was over anyway. Why not just throw in the towel?"

"Was your lawyer present?"

"I told them I didn't care about my defense. The truth was the truth. It was better to get it over with."

"Oh, Miranda, that was a *big* mistake."

"A mistake?"

He groans. "Did you say anything about me?"

"No. I refused to say anything about anyone else who was there. I'm not ratting on anyone. Why should I? I'm the one to blame. I'll take the heat."

"You're amazing, honey."

I sigh. Mitch has only called me *honey* a few times. Before, I'd always gotten such a rush out of it. Now it is meaningless.

"You've got to get an attorney, Miranda. Do you want me to find someone for you?"

"They said the court would appoint someone."

"No, no, you don't want a court-appointed attorney. You need someone good. I'll help you with it."

"Really?"

"Yes, but it'll have to be our secret, okay? Not that there's anything wrong with it. There isn't. But it might look suspicious. And you know they'll be pointing the finger at everyone for a while."

"Uh, Mitch . . ." I'm not sure how to tell him this.

"Yeah?"

"Detective Sanders told me the D.A. knows you were at the party."

He curses and I hear a loud thud, like maybe he dropped a tool or something on the floor of the bike shop. I imagine him there, wearing his biking pants. "What'd you say?" he asks in a quiet tone.

"I refused to answer. I told her that I wasn't willing to talk about anyone else. I said I could only tell her of my involvement."

"I wonder who they're talking to—besides you, that is."

"Well, obviously Kyra is talking to them." Just then I wonder if Kyra will ever talk to me again. Probably not.

"I'll contact an attorney I know and have him give you a call."

"Thanks, Mitch."

"It's going to be okay, Miranda. Just stay strong, and the whole thing will probably blow over in a week or two."

Stay strong? How can you *stay* something that you never were in the first place? But I don't voice my perplexing question. I would much rather Mitch continue to see me as his strong Greek goddess or even Celia from our play. Maybe somehow he *will* help rescue me from this terrible nightmare.

I'm sitting in the kitchen when Shelby gets home. It's the middle of the afternoon on a sunny spring day, and I'm not doing anything, just sitting at the table like a zombie. I don't even know how long I've been there.

"I'm exhausted," she announces as she dumps her wheeled bag in a corner of the floor and kicks off her shoes. "What a horrible flight. And it takes forever to go through security these days. I practically had to undress for them. I don't know why I don't just find another line of work that doesn't involve so much traveling." She opens the fridge and pulls out a beer, pops the tab, then turns toward me, as if she's just seeing me. "What's wrong with you? You look really awful."

I say nothing, just sit there dumbly, staring down at the shiny white tiles that cover the top of the small kitchen table that Shelby found on sale at BigMart last fall.

"Miranda?" I hear the irritation in her voice. "What's the matter with you? Are you sick or something? Should I be keeping my distance? I can't afford to get the flu, you know."

"Maybe you should sit down, Shelby."

"*Oh, no!*" she exclaims, pointing her index finger in the air like Sherlock Holmes. "I just knew this would happen. You got yourself knocked up, didn't you? And after all those lectures I've given you about birth control . . . I offered to get you the Pill, the Patch, whatever. I cannot believe you'd do this to me—"

"That's *not* it!" I stand up now, glaring down at her. "I only wish that *were* the problem. If me being pregnant could erase this thing, I would gladly have twins, quadruplets even—"

"Miranda Maria Sanchez!" Her eyes open so wide I can see the bloodshot white area all around the blue irises. It's obvious I have her full attention now. "What on earth is going on with you?"

I sink into the wooden chair, leaning my head forward till it hits the table with a dull thud.

I hear her pull out a chair, scraping across the old linoleum, and then she sits down. "I'm waiting."

I lift up my head and look at her. "Sammy is dead."

Her face is blank, expressionless. "Oh."

But the way she says it is like she doesn't even care. Or maybe she's relieved, like she thought it was something far worse. But what could that possibly be? "Did you hear me, Shelby? I just told you that *Sammy is dead.*"

"I heard you, Miranda. And I'm sorry. Really, I am. That must be quite a blow. You've known Sammy for years."

"Yeah. I feel horrible."

"What happened? Car wreck?"

"They're not totally sure yet. But, uh, Shelby . . ." I pause, searching for the right words. What are the right words? "He died . . . Sammy died here."

"What?"

"Yeah. Last night."

"Here? Right here, in my kitchen? Good grief!"
She glances around the small room as if she expects
to see blood or something.

"Actually he died in the living room."

She jumps up now and runs into the living room,
spilling her beer as she races around the corner. I
follow her, wondering if she thinks he might still
be there. "How on earth did this happen, Miranda?
I demand some kind of explanation."

"I'm trying to explain, if you'll just let me."

She sinks down on the couch now and takes a
long swig of beer, then narrows her eyes in my
direction. "Explain, Miranda. *Now!*"

"I had a little party last night—"

"Here? You had a party here while I was gone?"

"I didn't think you'd mind. And I cleaned everything all up before . . . and after."

"Well, okay. But what happened?"

"I asked Sammy to come, and he's not usually
into partying, you know."

"I assume you're saying this was a drinking
party, then."

I nod. "Yeah. Just beer and wine. No big deal.
We were celebrating the play, you know." I wait for
a reaction.

"Go on."

"Anyway, Sammy had a couple of beers. He
seemed like he was having fun. He danced and stuff
and then kind of passed out. I wasn't really paying
attention, but I swear all I saw him drink was a couple of beers. Well, that and water. But water never
hurt anyone."

"And then what?"

"Well, he was just kind of sitting there." I point to the sofa. "And then Kyra showed up—"

"She wasn't already here?"

"For some reason she hasn't really been into partying lately," I explain.

"*And . . . ?*"

"And Kyra thought Sammy didn't look so good. She thought something was wrong. And she wanted me to call 911."

Shelby rolls her eyes. "Great, get the cops over here—man, what a circus!"

"I didn't want to call, even when I realized that Sammy really was having a problem. So Kyra called. Everyone else took off then. By the time the paramedics got here, Sammy had already gone into cardiac arrest."

"Cardiac arrest?"

"That's what they said."

"But Sammy was in good shape—"

"Yeah, that's what I said too. But that's what they said it was. They're going to do an autopsy—"

"So, are you saying—" Shelby stands up and stares at her purple sofa. "You're telling me that Sammy James died right here, on this sofa?"

"Yeah, sort of. Or maybe on the floor . . . I'm not sure."

"Well, that's disgusting, Miranda. You throw a party without permission and then someone dies right here on my sofa. What kind of girl are you anyway?"

I don't answer. I just stand there and wait for the

rest. And she lets me have it too, one verbal blow after another, until she's finally spent and all out of ammunition. The weird thing is, I don't even care. In fact, I almost wish she'd pick up a stick and beat me or throw something at me. Maybe it would ease my pain. Then she storms off to her room and slams the door. Once again I'm all alone.

Oh, Sammy, where are you?

Instead of sleeping tonight, I replay every conversation I can remember having with Sammy. It's like running a movie theater through my mind. As if it brings him back somehow . . . or simply tortures me. I'm morbidly curious about how much pain a person can endure and yet survive. Thinking about Sammy induces enough pain to kill me, I'm sure. And yet I'm still alive. Barely.

I force myself to remember the night we built the snowman. The night of the snowy kiss. That's how I think of that night with Sammy. It's all etched into my brain in shades of black and white and red. Riding in his old red pickup, cutting cookies in the parking lot, trespassing to build the beer-bellied snowman, and then the kiss. The night of the snowy kiss. And yet I pushed him away.

Right after that night I started dating Ryan Emerson. Not that I especially liked Ryan, but he was a good distraction. Or maybe just a decoy. I'm not even sure now. But my plan had been twofold at the time. First, I thought it was a good way to distance myself from Sammy. Next, I hoped it would camouflage the fact that I was head over heels for our new English teacher. And it didn't hurt matters that Ryan was in Mitch's biking club. As was Sammy. And my basketball buddy Rebecca Landis. I even tried to get Sammy interested in Rebecca. I knew she had always been interested in him. It actually seemed like they had a lot in common.

But I must admit to feeling real pangs of jealousy when I saw those two together. It seriously bugged me that Sammy appeared to so easily desert me for another girl, even if I had been the one playing matchmaker. But then, Rebecca is a nice girl—in fact, she's a lot like Sammy. She's into sports and church and doing the right thing. They just seemed like a good pair. And it got Sammy off my case for a while. He seemed so concerned about me. He seriously thought I was turning into a "wild child." That's what he actually started calling me. Oh, not when anyone else could hear, of course, but when he wanted to get my attention. It was his way of reminding me that he thought I was being foolish.

Sammy and Rebecca didn't last very long though. According to her, he was the one to quit calling. I didn't ask him why. Didn't want to stir anything up. Besides, I was too busy strategizing new ways to get Mitch's attention without attracting the attention of others. It was a real challenge. Not so much getting his attention—that came pretty naturally. But doing it discreetly so other kids didn't notice, especially Kyra, since I strongly suspected she was doing the same thing. But we never spoke of it. When we did speak it was usually light and superficial. Sometimes I think Kyra is the queen of superficiality. At least, that's what she wants us all to believe. But I know for a fact she's quite deep. Maybe it's the deepness that scares her.

I honestly think Sammy was the only one who saw right through me—all along. Like I've said, he could read me like a book—a book with a bad ending. He knew from the start that I had a crush on Mitch. I still remember a time we were all riding over Beacon Hill. I'd had some difficulty with the steep incline to begin with, but after a couple weeks of biking I was able to soar to the top. On this particular day I took the lead, probably showing off for Mitch, but I knew Sammy was right on my heels.

Just as I crested the top, Sammy pulled up beside me, keeping perfect pace. "Hey," he called, but he appeared slightly troubled, like he was worried.

"What's up?"

He took in a breath. "You've got it bad for him, don't you, Randi?"

"Huh?" I glanced over at Sammy, still catching my breath. "You mean Ryan?"

Sammy shook his head, then sat up straighter on his seat. "You know who I mean." We were both slowly applying our brakes now as our bikes began to coast downhill.

But I still played dumb. "Who?"

"Mitch."

I laughed as I reached down for my water bottle. "Sure shooting, Sherlock! Wow, you're really on to something big." I rolled my eyes at him. "Like have you noticed that every single girl in Macon High's got it bad for Mr. Wonderful?"

"It's different with you, though."

I gave him my best bewildered expression. "What do you mean?"

"Mitch thinks *you're* hot too."

I threw back my head and guzzled a big swig of water. It dripped down my chin as I grinned at him. "Yeah, right!"

"I mean it, Randi. You should be careful."

Now I started laughing, really laughing. I tried to act like I was laughing at the total ridiculousness of his warning. But I was actually feeling silly and giddy, almost intoxicated by the mere suggestion that Mitch might find me attractive. And yet I was actually thinking that maybe Sammy was right. Maybe Mitch *did* think I was hot. But hey, that was just peachy with me!

Then I released my brakes and blasted down that hill, dangerously fast, leaving Sammy far behind. And that's how it continued between Sammy and me, the distance between us widening with each passing day. Oh, we still spoke and joked around, but it was *all* on the surface now. There was this wedge between us. I think I blamed Rebecca for the wedge for a brief time, until they broke up, but looking back, I can see it was really my doing. I kept pushing Sammy away from me. It kills me to think of that now.

But back then I was oblivious to a lot of things. I don't even remember for sure when Kyra really started pulling away from me. It's like one day we were good friends . . . and then we weren't. At first I thought she was simply stressed out. She's like that. Everything hits her extra hard. It's like she thinks she has to be perfect or something.

It might have to do with her parents. She says they expect too much of her. But I don't really see it. They seem pretty cool to me. I don't know how many times I've thought I would gladly take them over my situation. I remember one time when I actually said as much to Shelby, right in the middle of a big fight. "I wish you were more like Kyra's mom!" I had screamed at her.

Instead of getting furious, she just laughed. "Yeah, I'm sure you want a family just like *Ozzie and Harriet.*"

"Who are they?"

"Just this stupid old sitcom where everyone in the family was perfect."

"Well, it sure beats our family. If anything we're more like the Ozzy Osbourne family—only they're a lot more interesting."

She stuck her finger in my face. "Hey, I'd much rather be like *them*. At least they're for real. They don't go around hiding their stinking problems beneath a bunch of toothpaste smiles and a string of fake pearls."

I wasn't totally sure what she meant by that, but

it did make me wonder about the James family.
Maybe they weren't as perfect as they appeared.
Maybe they did put too much pressure on Kyra. The
funny thing was, Shelby actually packed me a lunch
the next morning. I was totally shocked and could
barely mumble thank you. Of course, the lunch was
horrible. But it was kind of sweet that she at least
tried.

Anyway, as Kyra continued to pull away from
me, I became suspicious that it had something to do
with Mitch. But back then I assumed everything had
to do with Mitch. I thought I was doing a great job
of covering up my real feelings. I continued dating
Ryan, and I'm absolutely certain I never acted as
obvious as girls like Brianna Devereaux. She literally
swooned every time Mitch entered the room. But
then Brianna has never been exactly subtle when
it comes to her relationships with guys. I'm sure she
saw Mitch as the potential catch of her high-school
career. Although what he'd see in her, besides a
plastic sort of beauty, is beyond me. Still, I honestly
don't think I ever acted as obvious as Brianna. Even
when Mitch made a big deal about me reading some
lines for the play and urged me to try out, I acted
like my only problem was plain old stage fright.
Actually, that wasn't just an act. The last thing I
ever wanted to do was stand on a stage and recite
lines from Shakespeare in front of an auditorium
of people.

But somehow, when I stood up in class and read
those first lines with Mitch reading right along with
me—a love scene even—it felt so natural, so right,

that I almost thought I could do it . . . for him. Of course, as soon as I finished, reality set in. But everyone, including Mitch, was so encouraging that I decided to give it a shot. I tried to convince myself it went with my New Year's resolution, kind of crazy and maybe even fun . . . if I didn't die of stage fright in the process.

It was Kyra's idea that Sammy and I practice together for tryouts. I'm still not sure why she did that. Maybe to get us both out of her hair. I think it was around this time that I first suspected something was seriously wrong with her. Something more than stress. I noticed how she sometimes seemed to be right on the edge, like if one more thing happened, she was going to snap. Then other times she was so checked out. Weird. I kept thinking I was going to talk to her about it, but then she has this amazing way of distancing you when you're trying to break through to her. As if she doesn't want you to get too close. She can joke and minimize a sticky situation until you start to think you're the one who has the problem. And so the gulf between Kyra and me kept growing wider and wider too.

During Sammy's and my first time of rehearsing our lines together, I decided to set him straight. "I want you to understand," I told him, "that just because we're doing this doesn't mean I want to hear your minisermons about my life, okay?"

His brows lifted in a slight feign of innocence. "Sure, whatever."

I looked him straight in the eye. "And not one word about Mitch, either."

"Hey, I didn't see a thing yesterday," he threw in.

"Huh?"

"When I walked into the bike shop right before our ride."

I felt my face redden as I remembered how Sammy had walked in right as Mitch's hand slid all the way down my back after he'd playfully pulled my ponytail.

"That's right," I snapped. "You *didn't* see a thing." But I knew by the angle of his brows that he was still telling me to watch my step, to be careful. Some things don't need words.

Fortunately, we soon forgot our differences as we became totally immersed in learning our lines. And Shakespeare is not easy. But perhaps the weirdest part was how neither of us had ever shown the slightest interest in theater before. In fact, we both disliked being the focus of attention. Well, unless it was in sports—that was different. Yet every time we practiced our lines, we both transformed into these totally different people—Celia and Oliver. We *became* our characters, only our characters seemed more real than our own true selves. How is that possible? I remember looking into Sammy's eyes, reciting my lines, and thinking—yes, honestly thinking, *Hey, I could love this guy.* As I think of this now, I'm afraid something within me is going to crack and explode and spew out hot molten pain. Strangely enough, I'm hoping it will kill me.

Oh, Sammy, where are you?

It's Monday, but I didn't go to school today. I phoned the attendance office and told Mrs. Colley that I'm sick. It's true. I am. Who would even question this? Shelby sure didn't. She just looked at me sitting like a stump on my bed, then shook her head and left. I want to call Detective Sanders, to ask her what the autopsy revealed, but I am too scared. I wonder if she's planning to call me anyway. And so I wait. I sit and then I pace and then I sit.

I haven't slept for two nights now. Not really. I suppose I may have dozed for a few minutes here and there, but then I wake up—bolt upright, with my heart racing like I've just biked up a mountain. Then I get up and walk around the apartment, with the lights off, simply listening. I wonder if Sammy might still be here. His ghost, I mean. I strain my ears to hear him, hoping that he's trying to tell me something. But all I hear is the ticking of Shelby's stupid Tweety Bird clock and the shushing sound of the street cleaner down below. As I tiptoe from room to room and back again, I begin to feel as if *I* am the ghost. *I* am the one who is dead. This is the only thought that brings some comfort.

But not in the daylight hours. When the night shadows are gone, I can see that I am flesh and bones, a living being, but not really. I haven't been able to eat anything since the party. Shelby actually seemed a little worried about me last night. She made a peanut-butter sandwich and told me I had to eat it. I thanked her and pretended to take a bite and slowly chew, but as soon as she turned away I spit it out, gagging as I did. I tried to drink the milk, but could only get a few swallows of those thick curds down my throat before I gave up and poured it down the sink.

Just before noon the phone rings, splitting the silence of the apartment like an ax. I don't pick it up. I simply listen as the machine does its thing. I expect it's that obnoxious reporter from the *Macon Herald*. He's already called a dozen times, leaving almost as many messages to call him back—"just to chat." I listen as Shelby's voice chirps out her perky greeting. But this is followed by a woman's voice, all business.

"This is Detective Sanders of Macon Police Department—"

I cut her off as I pick up the phone. "This is

Miranda," I say in a voice that sounds shaky, raspy from lack of use.

"I thought you might be there, Miranda. I wondered if I could get you to answer a few more questions for me this afternoon. Maybe we can put some closure on this case."

"Did the, uh, the report come in?" I can't bring myself to say the word *autopsy* aloud. It sounds so cold and clinical, like stainless steel and scalpels and white-clad strangers. Nothing that should have anything to do with my Sammy.

"Yes."

"Will you tell me—"

"Let's make a deal, Miranda. You come down to the station and answer my questions, and I'll fill you in on the report."

This woman knows how to get what she wants, I think. *She's good.*

"Okay." I agree to come down at one-thirty. Then I walk around the apartment and try to think, but my brain is not cooperating. I wonder if I should take a shower or brush my teeth, but then I don't know why it should matter whether I do or not. So I don't. I haven't had a shower since Saturday. Kyra would be seriously grossed out. But then I guess it doesn't matter anymore because I haven't talked to Kyra since . . . I bite my lower lip, now crusty and scabby and swollen from my recent lip-biting abuse. And try not to think about Sammy's family, or what they would say or possibly do to me if they could mete out their own form of justice.

The last time I saw Mr. and Mrs. James was the night of the play. As usual, they were dressed like something out of an advertisement. They seemed so happy—at least at first. They came up to me and congratulated me. "You were brilliant, Miranda!" Mr. James patted me on the back with a big smile. "We never knew you had it in you, old girl. But you really made us proud tonight."

How proud *I* was when he said those words! Especially since Shelby was away on her "important" business trip and hadn't seemed all that sorry to miss our only performance. Again I wished, as I had for so many years, that I could be part of the James family.

"Have you seen Sammy or Kyra?" Mrs. James' eyes darted across the crowded auditorium. "I've been looking everywhere but haven't spotted either of them since the curtain call."

"I'm not sure where Sammy took off to, but the last time I saw Kyra she was talking to Dylan back there." I pointed toward the stage. "Want me to go fetch the lovely Rosalind for you?"

Mrs. James smiled, but it was a tight little smile, the one she uses when all is not well. "Thank you."

Mr. James nodded crisply. "We'd appreciate that."

So off I went to find Kyra and tell her that her proud parents were waiting to congratulate her. I also reminded her, for about the tenth time, about my big party, but then she said something about going fishing instead. Certain she was joking, I went off in search of Sammy. But I still didn't see him anywhere. He had disappeared. That's when it occurred to me that he had seemed awfully eager to get out of the auditorium.

I'd spoken with him briefly right after our final scene, but that had been about 30 minutes earlier. He and Jamal and I had found a barrelful of old hula skirts and props that had been used in *South Pacific* a few years back. We did a little hula dancing backstage and general cutting up as we waited for the rest of the play to end. I guess I was feeling sort of high from having delivered my first real performance. Okay, I knew it wasn't a great performance, but simply having done it without any major mishaps was a huge milestone. And I was feeling pretty good about life in general. I suppose those few swigs I'd taken from Tyrone's flask were having a slight dizzying effect on me as well. He'd been sharing Hale Ramsey's "special mix" with everyone— well, everyone who was interested, that is. I'm not quite sure what was in that thing, but it had really cleared out my sinuses.

Anyway, I'd already given Jamal a big hug and kiss and was now going after Sammy. "We did it!" I said as I threw my arms around his neck and sloppily smacked him right on the cheek. "Aren't you glad?"

"I'm just glad it's over," he said in a less-than-enthusiastic voice.

I stepped back and peered at him. His face, dimly lit by the stage lights that reflected from the curtains, didn't look happy. "Man, Sammy, you should be feeling really good tonight. You just delivered a great performance." I poked him in the chest. "You and me, man, we were like the nobodies of drama, and look what we did tonight!"

He merely shrugged.

"Sammy—" I spoke more quietly—"you are way too glum for me, buddy."

"Sorry. It's the best I can do at the moment."

Then I smiled in a flirtatious way and slipped my arm around his waist. Snuggling up close, I said, "Aw, come on, Sammy. You can do better than this." I put my face next to his. "Why don't you come to my party tonight and try to lighten up? Just have some fun. Can't you see you're getting way too serious for everyone?"

"Is that what you guys say about me?"

I grinned and playfully twirled his stick-on mustache. "Well, of course, silly. What'd you think we'd say? But you must remember the old adage about all work and no play. You don't want to be a dull boy, do you, Sammy?" And then I actually kissed him again. Not on the lips, but close. Very close. Close enough for him to react.

He pulled me toward him, held me there a moment, then shook his head. "It's no use, Miranda."

I frowned. "No use?"

He peered down, as if he were really trying to see inside me. "You and me, Randi. We're too different."

At the time it seemed ironic that he'd say something like that. Especially since Kyra has said many times that Sammy and I are so much alike *we* should be the twins. But I just laughed. "Hey, you know what they say about opposites, don't you?"

He smiled—a sad sort of smile. "Yeah, well, you

know I'm attracted to you, Randi. That's never been a secret."

"Then come to my party tonight, Sammy. Just come and have fun. I promise I'll dance with you." I gave him a sideways glance. "And who knows what else?"

His face grew serious again. "Okay, I'll think about it."

"All right."

"Miranda!"

I glanced toward Mitch, who was motioning me to come over. "Gotta go, Sammy."

He frowned. "Yeah."

As it turned out, Mitch only wanted me to help Kyra with a rip in her costume that kept getting bigger and bigger. Quickly, I pinned it together, then hugged her before she got ready for her final scene. "You look mahvalous, dahling," I assured her while we waited in the wings for her next cue. . . .

Then, suddenly, I'm back in the present. I hear the phone ringing again, screaming like a wounded bird. Thinking it's the detective, I jump to get it. "Hello?"

"Miranda, how are you doing?"

I recognize his voice immediately. It's the kind of warmth that pulls you right in. "Mitch? Where are you?"

"At school. Actually I'm standing in the faculty parking lot. I'm on my cell. It's my lunch hour."

"Oh." I try to imagine school, lunchtime. It seems like something from another galaxy. Or something that used to happen back when I was a different person.

"I just wanted to hear how it's going." He pauses. "I noticed you weren't here today. But then, neither was Kyra."

"Yeah." I try to imagine Kyra at school, wearing her purple cheerleader outfit and doing a back flip. But it all seems so unreal, impossible. Like a bad joke, or a long-forgotten place we can never return to.

"Have you heard from the police? Have they questioned you again?"

"I'm going in this afternoon."

"I spoke to the lawyer I mentioned. He sounded interested. I gave him your number. Has he called?"

"No."

"You better call him." Then Mitch tells me a name and a number, and I say uh-huh and act like I'm writing it down. But I'm not. I'm just standing there gazing out the front window at the cherry tree. My grandpa—a man I've never met—planted it there when he was a little boy. It's as tall as the peak of the roof now and full of white blossoms. Now they're unbearably cheerful.

"Let me know how it goes, okay?"

"Sure."

"There's a rumor going around the school."

"I figured."

"Kids are saying Sammy took Ecstasy."

"Ecstasy?" I frown. "Where would he get that?"

"Oh, it's everywhere."

"Yeah, I know that. But, I mean, why would

Sammy have something like that? Why would he take it?"

"You never know."

"Yeah, I guess not."

"Keep me informed, okay?"

"Yeah. I'll try."

"Thanks, honey."

"Uh-huh." Then I hang up. It's weird. If Mitch had called me last week, I'd have been totally thrilled. Now I just feel numb.

"Ecstasy?" I say the word aloud. It tastes bitter, foreign in my mouth. Of course I know what the drug is, even though I never saw the stuff until this year, after I decided to become a partyer. Still—and amazingly—I never took any of it myself. I'm not totally sure why. The first time I saw those little pastel-colored flowers and smiley faces, I actually thought they were candy! Ryan had teased me and assured me that they were as harmless as candy. But I wasn't too sure. And my gut told me I couldn't entirely trust Ryan.

Then there was that night when Kyra and I saw Brianna on the stuff. The silly girl was making a complete fool of herself as she gushed over everyone like she was the love princess. I'm pretty sure she went to bed with Hank, another senior, that night too. I can't even imagine how she felt the next day. Anyway, I'd sworn to myself, then and there, that I'd never touch the stuff. Drinking was one thing, but Ecstasy was another.

Perhaps Mitch is right. Maybe a part of me is seriously repressed. That's what he likes to call it—

repressed. I didn't particularly care for the sound of that word at first. For one thing it rhymes with depressed. But worse than that, it conjures up this stiff-collared image of a prudish librarian, like Miss Tristen at our school. She acts as if the school library is some sort of religious sanctuary that she's been appointed to uphold and protect. But in my battle against repression, I've read some of the writings of Mitch's favorite philosophy gurus—guys like Jung and Nietzsche. Sometimes the opinions they express not only make me feel *re*pressed but *de*pressed.

I've raised my concerns about this with Mitch, since we discuss these things from time to time. But maybe I don't care as much as I try to seem to care. Perhaps it's just one of the little tactics I've used to get his attention in the past few months. He seems to get off on the idea that he's converting me from this uptight, repressed teenager into a free-spirited wild woman. Perhaps I might turn into someone like Shelby! And yet it's that very possibility that has kept me from going completely over the edge. So far anyway. Who's to say what will happen to me now? But it used to be I'd look at the way she lives her life and just shudder. All I knew was that I didn't want to become like that. I know it's not a terribly loving way to perceive your own flesh-and-blood mother. But it's the truth—at least, it used to be. Now I'm thinking that Shelby, with all her many and varied faults, has never screwed up her life as badly as I have done recently. Maybe she's a good role model after all.

At 1:00 I slowly walk toward City Hall. As
I cross Main Street, I ask myself the same question
that's been floating around my head since Mitch's
phone call. *Why in the world would Sammy take
Ecstasy? Why, why, why?*

It's possible this stupid rumor isn't true. I know
how these crazy things can start out small and
then spread like wildfire at school. Sometimes they
contain a drop of truth, but it's usually diluted in
an ocean of lies. But why would they say Ecstasy?
That is so un-Sammy-like. "Wrong, in so many
ways," as he would say. And yet, if my memory is
any clearer now, I do recall Sammy dancing a lot,
really cutting loose—not just with me, either, but
with *everyone*—guys and girls alike. It was pretty
weird . . . and very unSammylike.

When I push open the thick glass door and walk into City Hall, it feels like someone has tied heavy weights around my legs. I realize it *could* be true that Sammy took Ecstasy. After all, he wasn't himself that night. But still I wonder *why?* And then I see them.

Mr. and Mrs. James and Kyra. They are coming out of an office with a man and a woman, who are wearing suits. Even in my split-second glimpse, I can see that all three of the surviving Jameses' faces look pale, tired, and blank—as if their facial muscles have been cut and all their features are just hanging there. It's not the detective's office they're exiting from, but another office down another hall-way marked Justice Department. I'm not sure if they see me or not, but I turn and keep my head low as I duck toward a nearby drinking fountain. There I stay hunkered down, waiting with a pounding heart until they pass. I cannot bear to have them look at me. I'm certain their eyes alone can slice me into shreds, or simply shoot through my heart like a bullet and kill me. But would that really be so bad?

"Is that you, Miranda?"

I look up to see Detective Sanders. The James family is nowhere in sight now. So I stand up straight and push the dirty, tangled hair from my face. I casually walk toward her and say, "Hey," like she's some good friend at school. Like Taylor or Rebecca.

Then we are sitting in her office again. It's weird how something so normally foreign to my world should suddenly look so familiar. It's like I even know how many tile squares are on the floor, and the way their color pattern of green, black, and gray appears to be random but really is not.

"How are you doing, Miranda?"

I examine the hands lying limp in my lap. My nails are completely chewed off now, and the cuticles are red and peeling, close to bleeding. If I keep on chewing them, will my fingernails just disappear altogether? Will I just have round red nubs on my fingertips?

"You don't look too good."

I shrug. "Don't feel too good."

"Can I ask you a question, Miranda, strictly off the record?"

"Off the record?"

"I promise."

I shrug again.

"Do you do drugs?"

I look up at her, straight into her dull brown eyes, and answer honestly, "Not yet."

She begins thumbing through her file. "Let's see, where should we begin." But it's not a question, simply a statement. "All right, how about if I tell you about the autopsy report?"

"Okay." I sit straighter in my chair now, trying to focus my attention—tuning my ears and my eyes so I can really listen.

"I won't go into all the medical mumbo jumbo. Basically it says that Samuel's blood alcohol level was less than 3 percent." She glances up. "That's probably those couple of beers you mentioned. But his blood test also revealed high levels of methylated ampheta—"

"What's that?"

"It's an amphetamine. An 'upper,' also known as MDMA or Ecstasy. And he didn't die of cardiac arrest as the paramedics first suspected."

"What then?"

"It's called *hyponatremia* and is a result of hyperthermia—"

"Hypothermia?"

"No, hy*per*thermia. That's elevated body temperature."

"But Sammy wasn't hot. I mean, it was pretty warm in the apartment that night, but Sammy felt cold when I touched his face." I remember wrapping Shelby's throw around him and trying to warm his hand on my face, but I don't mention this.

"Sanders?" A man sticks his head in her door. "Sorry to disturb you, but could you help us with the Ashford case?"

She stands. "Will you excuse me, Miranda? This should only take a few minutes."

I nod absently. My mind is back on Saturday night, trying to understand how it was that Sammy could've died of hyperthermia when he felt so cold. It just makes no sense. . . .

■   ■   ■

It was a soft spring evening when we left the auditorium after the play—not too hot, not too cold. Jamal gave me a ride home that night. It was so nice out that I even briefly considered holding the party down in the backyard. But I knew that Mr. Campton, our only tenant, lives in an apartment with a kitchen window that looks right out into the backyard. And although the old guy is half deaf, I wasn't so sure I wanted him to actually watch my friends and me as we partied and danced under the moonlight. So I kept to my original plan. Jamal stuck around and gave me a hand with things. His donation for the evening was a whole case of beer that his older brother had purchased for him. He packed the cans into our refrigerator and then went to check out our music selection. "Hey, you've got some good dancing CDs here," he told me as he started lining up some of Shelby's favorite disco CDs.

"Should we make more room for dancing?" I asked as I glanced around the small living room. I imagined myself actually dancing with Mitch. And why not? We were going to celebrate—to have fun. I was going to show him—maybe even *prove* to him—that I wasn't nearly as repressed as he thought.

"Yeah, let's push that couch back against the wall," suggested Jamal. "And move that table and lamp."

Just as we got the room rearranged, D.J. and Tressa walked in.

"This the right place?" asked D.J. as he handed me a six-pack of bottles. Then he dumped a bag of ice into the sink to create a cooler of sorts.

"Was it that hard to find?" I'd purposely left the

front door open downstairs with a sign that said Come On Up! Not only that, but I'd spent a good part of my morning digging out several strings of brightly colored Christmas lights and then winding them all the way up the two flights of stairs that lead to our apartment.

"Nah," said D.J. as he set a grocery bag on the counter. "We just thought we might find Santa up here."

"Yeah," said Tressa as she handed me a cheap jug of wine. "Merry Christmas!"

Jamal had the music thumping now, and I started handing out beers. Then I popped a tab and held up my can in a celebratory toast. "Here's to a great night!" I said loudly.

"Let the fun begin," Tressa added.

And so it did. Kids kept on coming. Some from the play, some not. I didn't even know who some of them were. But it didn't matter. We were one big happy family. It bothered me a little that Kyra wasn't making an appearance. I thought about what she'd said about fishing and wondered what was up with that. Then, to everyone's surprise, Sammy walked in, just as cool as you please. Kids greeted him—some razzed him in a teasing way, while others, like me, were genuinely glad to see him.

"Hey, Oliver!" I called to him from the kitchen, using his character's name.

"Celia," he tossed back to me. "What's up?"

"Just the greatest little party in town." I poured a bag of chips into a big wooden bowl. "Wanna beer? Just one?" I held a can out to him.

"Sure, why not," he finally agreed. "I s'pose it's not as bad as some things."

Then things got busy again, and I was occupied with playing hostess and trying to keep the food and drinks flowing. About an hour into the party, Mitch showed up. He'd changed since the play and looked pretty cool in a charcoal T-shirt and jeans. He usually dressed down slightly when he was hanging with us outside of school. Not that he came to all our parties. That would have been weird. But occasionally he encouraged us to get together to discuss a book or movie or whatever, and then he almost always showed up. But those were quieter gatherings, and if there was any drinking going on, it was usually just wine and things stayed pretty low-key. I always felt so grown-up during those times. I think that's why so many of us love Mitch— he treats us like adults.

When Mitch walked in, he captured most of my attention—as well as that of every other female present. And the party seemed to kick itself up a notch or two. The laughter got louder and the music sounded better. But Mitch is just like that. He took turns dancing with the girls, so I made sure I had a partner too. I suppose I hoped I could make Mitch jealous. First, I asked Sammy, but he turned me down, claiming—and not surprisingly— that he had two left feet. So I handed him another beer, then danced with Jamal and eventually D.J., who really does have two left feet. Then, just as I was starting to feel seriously neglected by Mitch, he grabbed me by the hand and pulled me out onto the floor with him. I've never considered myself much of a dancer, and Kyra says I have the natural rhythm of a baked potato, but when I danced with Mitch, it felt like I was finally doing it right. He seemed to think so too, because he danced the next *two* dances with me.

I was pretty light-headed by then—partially frombeing so close to Mitch, but also because I'd been drinking fairly liberally without having had any food to speak of. As we danced a slow number, I wished the song would go on forever. It was around then that I noticed Sammy had really livened up—a lot. Instead of having two left feet, he was moving so fast I could've sworn he had four or five feet. But I might have been getting a little blurry by then.

Anyway, I danced a couple of times with Sammy, who seemed to be having a good time. But things were relatively wild and loud by then too. When I went to the kitchen to clear my head and catch my breath, I was pleasantly surprised to see that Mitch had followed me. He helped himself to some sort of drink. I can't remember what kind now. Then we stood around and talked—and flirted— for a while. Kids came in and out of the kitchen pretty regularly, and that bugged me. I wanted to be alone with Mitch. But everyone seemed to be thirsty or hungry or both. Sammy got one of Shelby's big workout drink cups from the cupboard—a 32-ounce one—and kept filling it with water and ice from the sink.

"Man, you must be really thirsty," I said on what

seemed like his tenth trip. I was fairly certain he was just coming in and out to keep an eye on Mitch and me. Same old Sammy.

But he tossed me a goofy grin and said, "Hey, when you're hot you're *hot!* And my dancin' is hot! Why doncha open a window or something, Randi? It's like 100 degrees in here."

I threw back my head and laughed. "Well, Sammy boy, if you can't take the heat, you better get outta my kitchen."

"Come on, Sammy," shrieked Tressa as she grabbed his arm. "It's my turn to dance with you."

And so it went, kids coming and going, me playing the slightly inebriated hostess and flirting shamelessly with Mitch. Unfortunately it wasn't long before a couple other girls joined us in the kitchen. But I could tell Mitch liked the extra attention. I'm sure it's his favorite setting. Him, acting like the expert on all things important in life, surrounded by several good-looking, wide-eyed girls. I tried not to show that it bugged me. Tried to act mature—after all, I was the host of this totally cool party.

I don't recall what time it was when I first noticed that Sammy had conked out. I laughed when I saw him flopped back on the sofa against the wall, with Shelby's bright-colored cup still grasped loosely in his hand. I hadn't seen him consume more than a couple of beers, but I knew he wasn't used to alcohol, and maybe he was just tired. Besides it was pretty late. Later than I'd even imagined, as it turned out. . . .

■　■　■

Detective Sanders' voice jolts me back to the present. "Sorry, Miranda, that took longer than I'd expected." She picks up the folder. "Where were we?"

I blink and force myself to return to the moment. But my mind feels blank and empty now. Not only that, but there's a constant buzz in my head. It's been there since Sunday morning, but the volume increases by the hour.

She says the word I cannot say. "The autopsy . . . you had a question about hyperthermia?"

Now I remember. *Hyperthermia.* "No way," I tell her with the kind of conviction that I actually feel might bring Sammy back. "It might've been warm in the apartment that night with everyone dancing and all–" I vigorously shake my head–"but Sammy felt almost cold just before the paramedics arrived. Not only that, he'd been guzzling gallons of ice water. So he couldn't have been overheated. It's impossible."

"Yes, we know. Hyperthermia was merely the beginning of his trouble. There's another part to this." She scans the paper in her hand. "The scientific term is *induced acute hyponatremia,* but what it really means is that Samuel had too much fluid in his body. Specifically in his brain stem. The medical term is *cerebral edema.*"

"But how can that–?"

"It's something that comes with the whole Ecstasy territory." She studies me closely. "You say you've never taken this drug?"

I shake my head, then wish I hadn't because the motion makes me feel nauseated.

"Ecstasy elevates your body temperature. Depending on the dosage and the person, it can go as high as 108 degrees—"

"But Sammy was so cold." I'm more fuzzy and confused now.

"Right. But that was later on. You said yourself that the apartment was warm, and I assume that kids were dancing, right? Samuel too?"

I nod.

"All that activity, combined with the effects of the drug, can produce an amazing amount of body heat that makes the user incredibly thirsty."

"Oh."

"Kids who are experienced with this particular drug usually know that you need to drink water to cool off, but at the same time you have to be careful not to drink *too* much water."

"Why is that a problem?"

"Too much water can kill you."

"Huh?"

"Your body can only absorb so much fluid. Under normal circumstances, like if you're not impaired, you know when to stop drinking fluids. But in the case of drug impairment, you're not thinking normally. You feel thirsty, so you just keep drinking. Imagine someone overfilling a balloon. What happens?"

I cringe.

"Does that make sense now, Miranda?"

Unfortunately, it does. I nod without speaking.

"Does that sound like what may have happened to Samuel? Did you notice him consuming a lot of water?"

I nod again, but the buzz in my head is getting louder now.

"All right. Both you and Samuel's family have verified that he was *not* the kind of kid to use drugs, or even alcohol, as a rule. Is this true?"

"Yes."

"But he did drink a couple of beers that evening, right?"

"Only after I encouraged him."

"Do you think it's possible that the effect of the beers removed his normal inhibition to drugs? Do you think it's possible that he thought he'd give drugs a whirl just for the fun of it?"

I consider this. "I don't really think so. Sammy is—I mean he *was* a pretty big guy. I don't see how two beers would make him get *that* loose."

"Do you think he would recognize an Ecstasy pill if someone handed it to him?"

"You mean, like know it was a drug?"

"Right."

"I don't see why," I explain. "I thought it was candy the first time—"

"I thought you said you never—"

"The first time someone *offered* it to me. Just because I never used any doesn't mean I haven't had opportunities." I glare at her now.

"Yes, I'm sure it's readily available."

"For sure."

"Has it been going on for quite a while?"

"I don't really know. I was never into partying that much. Not until a few months ago." I sigh. "It was my New Year's resolution . . . to have fun."

"And have you?"

I swallow hard without answering.

"Well, Macon's a small town, and as far as we know there haven't been any other incidents involving this particular drug. That may be why the paramedics were caught off guard. But I transferred here last year from a place where it was getting to be fairly common. It appears to be a straightforward case to me."

I still say nothing. I don't want to be here in the police station anymore. I don't want to be anywhere. I wish I could just disappear—completely.

"Okay, let's get back to that night. Samuel obviously got the pill or pills from someone at your party. Do you think he took them knowingly?"

"You mean, do I think someone slipped them to him without him knowing? Like as a joke or a mean trick?"

She frowns now. "Well, I guess that's not quite what I mean. I realize the tablets look like candy, but the drug has a pretty strong taste."

I put my head in my hands and groan. "I don't know what happened that night. I don't know who might've given that crud to Sammy. But I do know Sammy never would've taken it if he hadn't come to my party."

"Will you give me a list of names now, Miranda?" I consider this. "I don't know."

"But someone at your party is partially, maybe

even mostly, responsible for your friend's death. Can't you see that?"

"Yeah." I look her in the eyes. "Me. I can see it's *me.*"

Clearly exasperated now, the detective exhales loudly through her nostrils. I can understand how she feels. "Look, Miranda, it's noble that you want to take all the blame for your friend's death yourself. But it's just not that simple. We need you to cooperate. Do you understand what it is . . . ?"

Suddenly her office feels like a fish tank. Like everything is underwater . . . as if her computer and telephone and pencils and the papers on her desk are all floating around. I'm floating too. I try to hear what she's saying, but her words get garbled in my head. I try to say something, but nothing comes out. I start to stand, but the buzzing in my head is growing so loud it drowns out everything else. Then I see dark splotches that grow bigger and steadily devour everything until all is black and silent.

Am I dead?

Oh, Sammy, where are you?

When I return to life, I am lying on some sort of vinyl-covered table, like in a doctor's office. Detective Sanders and another woman are standing over me. I blink and start to sit up, embarrassed.

"Hang on there a minute," commands the other woman as she removes a blood-pressure device from my arm.

"You fainted," says the detective. "This is Nurse Chandler. She takes care of our inmates."

"When did you last eat?" asks the nurse.

I sit up. "Can't remember."

Now a guy in uniform comes in, carrying a paper cup. "Here you go."

"Drink this orange juice," says the nurse. "I think you're just experiencing low blood sugar, but we can take you to the hospital if you like."

I feel my eyes widen. "No, I'm fine. Really." I take a sip of the juice. The citric acid burns my chapped lips, burns all the way down. But I force myself to empty the cup. I do *not* want to go to the hospital. Shelby would throw a fit, since our insurance coverage is pretty minimal.

"You need to take better care of yourself," warns the nurse.

"I know you feel badly about Samuel," says Detective Sanders. "But it won't do any good to ruin your health. Have you called that counselor yet?"

"No. But I will," I lie.

"Feeling any better now?" asks the nurse.

"Yeah." I swing my feet over the side of the table and stand. "I feel fine. I just forgot to eat breakfast is all."

"And lunch." Detective Sanders frowns at her watch. "I want you to think about making me that list."

"List?"

"Of everyone at your party."

"Oh."

"I better get back," says the nurse.

"Thanks." I try to smile, but I'm sure it looks pitiful.

"Can you do that?" asks the detective. "For Sammy?"

I notice that she didn't call him Samuel this time, but still I don't answer.

"Sammy would be alive right now if he hadn't taken that drug, Miranda. Those two beers you gave him didn't kill him. Of course, you kids shouldn't be drinking. But that's *not* what did it. Someone at your party gave him one, possibly two, Ecstasy tablets. And in the last several months, we know that someone has been flooding Macon with drugs. They're everywhere. We're looking for the supplier so we can stop the flow. We don't want that person selling more drugs to your friends. That's who bears the most guilt in my mind."

"So that makes me innocent?" I hear the sarcastic tone in my voice.

"Fine, if you want to go there." Detective Sanders leans forward. "You did have an underage drinking party. That was wrong and illegal. But to be fair, I guess we're all to blame. Our whole drug-taking, alcohol-drinking society."

I try to absorb all this, but it's too out there. All I know is that if I hadn't urged Sammy to come to my stupid party and have a couple beers, he'd still be alive. That seems pretty simple to me.

"So will you do it?"

"Make you a list?" I ask.

She nods.

"Maybe. At least I'll think about it."

As we walk down the hallway, she says, "You know you can't do anything about your friend's death now. But by making this list you could prevent something like this from happening again."

I'm not too sure about that. Right now I'm not sure about anything. But I nod like I understand, like she's talked some sense into me after all. And

then I get out of there and walk toward home. I
take the backstreets, worried that I might run into
someone from school, someone who might look at
me funny or ask questions. I wonder how long I
can hide out. Should I just drop out of school? Get
my GED and get out of this town? Maybe Mitch
would like to run away with me. Yet even that
fantasy fails to raise my spirits.

I'm only a few blocks from Nana's nursing
home. I know I won't run into any of my friends
there, so I decide to pay her a visit. Maybe I can
stay there with her—hide out in her room, lay low
until this whole thing blows over. Or until I blow
away. I wish I could just blow away.

I find her sitting outside in the courtyard. I carry
a white plastic chair over to her and sit down.

She peers at me. "Do I know you?"

I shrug.

Then she reaches over and touches my arm.
"Are you sad?"

I think I see a glimmer of recognition in her
eyes. "I am very sad."

"Why are you so sad, dear?"

"My friend died."

Her eyes shadow with concern. "I'm so sorry.
But at least your friend is safe with God now. Still,
it's terrible to lose a loved one."

"Yes." I search her face as a tiny ray of hope
races through me.

"I lost my husband, you know."

"Yes, I know," I say softly.

"Did you know him?"

"No." I know that my grandpa died when Shelby was still a girl. "I wasn't even born then."

"Of course you were born. He only died a year ago."

"Oh."

"Do I know you?" Her brows draw together now. It's the exact same expression she always used on me when I was little and she caught me doing something like sneaking candy before dinner.

"I'm Miranda."

"Don't know anybody named Miranda."

"Right." I bite into my thumbnail.

"But tell me, *Miranda,* how did your friend die?"

I peer into her eyes, wishing I could see her in there. "I killed him, Nana."

She blinks and pulls her pink sweater more tightly around her. Glancing around, as if for help, she stands and quickly walks away from me—as if she's in actual danger. As if I am a murderer.

And maybe I am. I leave the nursing home and go straight to the apartment. I'm barely through the door when the phone begins to ring. I go to the phone and, feeling like I barely have the strength to pick up the receiver, I answer.

"Hello?"

I can tell it's Mitch. But for the first time ever I don't want to speak to him.

"Miranda?"

"Yeah."

"Did I wake you?"

"I wish."

"You sound awful."

"Uh-huh."

"How did it go with the police?"

"I don't know."

"Did they tell you anything? Like the cause of Sammy's death?"

"Hyperthermia and another medical word that sounds sort of like that."

"What?"

"From the Ecstasy," I say with exasperation. "He got too hot and then too thirsty and—"

"Oh yeah. He *was* drinking a lot of ice water that night, wasn't he? I'd almost forgotten that."

"So you know about *that?*"

"What?"

"How Ecstasy makes you hot and thirsty . . ."

"Everybody knows that."

"*I* didn't know that. And obviously Sammy didn't either."

"That's too bad."

Too bad, I'm thinking. *Too bad?* Those two tiny words don't even begin to cover it!

"Did they ask about me?"

"No."

"Really?"

I honestly don't recall Mitch's name being mentioned. "No, they didn't say anything about you."

I hear him sigh. "Like I said, give it a week or two. It'll all blow over."

Still I say nothing. I begin to wonder if I'm really on the phone at all. Could I possibly be dreaming?

"Miranda? You still there?"

"Barely."

"You need to get some rest."

"I can't sleep. It's hopeless."

"Do you have anything to help you?"

"Help me?"

"To sleep. Like in your medicine cabinet. Like some over-the-counter sleep aid. I'll bet your mom has something."

I walk into the bathroom and look. "There's a bunch of stuff in the medicine cabinet," I tell him. "But I don't see anything for sleep."

"How about prescriptions? Your mom might have something from a doctor. It's not unusual. Any prescription bottles in there?"

I've seen Shelby's various prescriptions over the years, but I've never paid much attention to them. "Yeah, but I don't know what they're for."

"Well, it'll say on the label. Just read them."

Then the typed words *use for sleep* catch my eye. I pick up the bottle and read the label. "Ambien?"

"Bingo! Take one of those and call me in the morning."

"Right now? It's only four o'clock."

"It's up to you. But I'm sure you're exhausted from all this."

"Yeah." I set the bottle back on the shelf and shut the door. Then I see my face reflected in the mirror and halt, in shock. It's like I'm a total stranger. My skin is pale and taut. Dark shadows rim my eyes. My lips are cracked and chapped, and my hair looks like a fright wig. I stare at myself in fascination— like someone who sees a bad car wreck and can't take her eyes off the bodies strewn across the road.

"Miranda?"

I'm jerked back to reality. "Yeah."

"I have to go, honey. The guys will be here for our ride any minute now."

"Oh yeah." I can't imagine getting onto my bike right now, let alone into my Lycra biking pants. Just the thought of it makes me more tired.

"Take a pill and go to sleep. Maybe take a second pill to your bedroom with you, in case you wake up too soon. It's only Ambien. It can't hurt you."

"Uh-huh."

"Take care."

Then he hangs up. Instead of taking a pill, I go into the kitchen. I know that I need to eat something, but everything in the fridge looks like wood to me. I take out an apple and study it. I wonder how my teeth can possibly penetrate its surface. I set it down and open the front door. The afternoon paper is on our doorstep. We're a small town and the paper only comes three days a week. And not on Sunday.

I pick up the paper and walk to the table, my eyes locking onto the bold headline but avoiding Sammy's photo. Murder in Macon?! Local Teen Dies of Drug Overdose. Well, according to the detective, that's not exactly accurate. But then, this is a newspaper. Who expects them to get their facts straight? I sit down, open the paper, and begin to read. At first I am surprised to read my name, but then I remember I'm no longer a juvenile—no protection once you hit 18. In the paper or in the courts. I am listed as the "young woman who hosted the drinking party where Samuel James allegedly ingested a lethal dose of methylated amphetamines, otherwise known as Ecstasy." Still not quite accurate, but it appears they got the substance right. Most of the article is about how Sammy was an honor student, a respected athlete, and how things like this never happen in our town. One particular sentence holds my attention. "The district attorney is holding a wrongful death investigation. But if enough evidence is found, this could be upgraded to manslaughter— or even murder."

So there it is, in plain black and white. Murder. I fold the paper and sigh. It's only a matter of time now. The phone rings again, and I don't even move. It's probably that stupid reporter again. I wait for Shelby's greeting to pass, then listen.

"Hey, Miranda, this is Taylor. I'm worried about you. Are you there? Pick up if you're there."

So I pick up the phone. "Hello."

"Miranda." Her voice sounds relieved. "I'm so sorry about this. I know you really loved Sammy."

For the first time since this whole nightmare began, I feel a tightness in my throat, like I'm about to cry. But I don't. "Yeah, I did."

"And I'm sure you're feeling awful."

"Yeah."

"I want you to know I'm praying for you. Dylan is too. We know this must be devastating for you."

I wonder if they really know *how* devastating.

"If there's anything I can do, I mean *anything* . . . or if you just wanna talk . . ."

"Uh-huh."

"Well, I'm here for you. You know? I really am, Miranda."

"Thanks."

"I don't wanna bug you. I just want you to know, okay? I'm here for you. I'm praying."

"Thanks." I almost feel like I *could* talk to her. Pour out my story, my sadness, maybe even cry. But something holds me back. I'm afraid if I begin to let it out, it'll keep going and going—forever. And I'm just not ready for that.

"Do you think you'll be in school tomorrow?"

I sigh. "I don't know."

"Well, it's all anyone talked about today. They've got counselors on hand—for grief, you know. Kids were crying and everything. It was so sad. They'll have the counselors there all week. If you come to school, you could talk to one of them. A woman from my church is there. She's really cool, just out of college. Her name is Andi Pierce. I could introduce you—"

"Thanks. I've already got the name of a counselor . . . if I decide to go, that is."

"Right." Taylor pauses, and I wonder if I've offended her. "You really should go, Miranda. I think it'd help you to work through this stuff."

"Uh-huh."

"And, if you can, you should try to pray too. You know, God's really listening, Miranda. And he loves you."

Yeah, sure. God loves me. That's a good one, I think. But I just say, "Uh-huh," again. Like that's become my perfect answer to everything. It seems to work.

"Okay, I'll let you go. But *please* call me if you want to talk. Really."

"Uh-huh."

Then I hang up and open the refrigerator again. I take out the milk and get out a box of Cheerios. Somehow, after hearing Taylor's voice I think I can eat some cereal. It's weird, really, but I try not to think about it too much. I pour the cheerful little golden circles into a blue bowl, then douse them in milk, taking my time to sprinkle them with sugar. I take a bite and try not to think about how they taste like sawdust. Somehow I manage to eat most of them and then pour the remains into the garbage—like Cheerios rejects.

I consider turning on the TV and zoning out for a while, but it's time for news now. Local news first. And after reading the paper I don't think I can handle it. I'm glad Macon doesn't have its own TV station, or I'd probably have a bunch of television cameras at my door. Instead I go to my room and sit on my bed. I even try lying down, closing my eyes, and pretending that I'm asleep. Maybe I can trick myself.

But it's no use. And then Shelby comes home and stands outside my door. When I look up, I see the *Macon Herald* hanging loosely in her hand.

"Did you see this?" she asks in an irritated voice.

I sit up and rub my eyes, as if she woke me up from some deep slumber. "What?"

"The paper? Did you read what they said about you?"

I nod. "Yeah."

She rolls her eyes. "Well, I hope this is the worst of it, Miranda. My job's tough enough without having to go around explaining crud like this every other day."

"Sorry." I don't expect her to feel bad for me. I know that Shelby's world, for the most part, revolves around Shelby. No reason for that to change now.

"Did you eat yet?"

"Yeah."

"Good. I think I'll go out. I need to pick up some things at the mall. You need anything?"

Yeah, a gun so I can go shoot myself.

But I don't say this aloud. And besides, I wouldn't have the guts to do something that violent and bloody. I hear her in her bedroom, probably changing out of her work clothes. Then I hear the door slam and I know I am alone again.

I lie back down on my bed and stare at the Beatles poster—the one where they're wearing Nehru jackets and wire-rimmed glasses. They look sort of serious and sad, like they knew it would be only a matter of time until half of them were gone. I probably like Paul McCartney the best. I admire his ability to survive so much and still be creative. It occurs to me that Kyra gave me that poster, shortly after I gave her one of John Lennon. We were both into the Beatles back then. Or at least I was.

I wonder what Kyra is doing right now. Has she been able to cry? What will she do without Sammy? As different as those two were, they were still very close. I used to envy that. Now I wonder if she could possibly miss him more than I do. If so, she must be dying too. I suppress the urge to run for the phone, to call her. I know she won't want to talk to me. I hope in time that will change. But I don't really see how.

That buzzing sound in my head is back now. I think about the Ambien in the medicine cabinet. I think about Mitch's advice. He's a grown-up. A teacher even. It's almost like having a doctor prescribe it. And after all, I'm sure my doctor would, if I had the nerve to go in and tell him what was wrong. But the mere idea of sitting in his office and having him peer down at me over his bifocals is unnerving.

I go to the bathroom and open the cabinet. I shake out a pill. So tiny. How could it possibly be harmful? And why should I care?

I peer into the bottle and try to calculate how many are in it. It's about one-third full. Shelby must actually use these to help her sleep. Who knew? I'm guessing there might be 20, maybe 30 left. Would that be enough to end my pain?

I carry the bottle to the kitchen and carefully pour the pills out onto the tile-topped table. I line them up in the grout line so they don't roll away and then count them. There are 26. Surely that would be enough to end this thing. I imagine how blissful it would feel to go to sleep—and then to just sleep forever.

I go to the sink for a glass of water. Then I wonder if milk might not be better. It might help to keep them from upsetting my stomach. I don't like the idea of Shelby coming home in time to see me puking up her pills into the toilet. I can imagine her saying, "I can't believe you wasted all my pills, Miranda. Don't you know how much those things cost? And our insurance doesn't even cover prescriptions!"

I fill a tall glass with milk. I saw on a movie once where the woman took pills slowly, one at a time. I wonder if that's the right way to do this thing. I set the glass on the table and then consider writing a note. But to whom? Shelby? And what would I say? "Sorry I wasn't a better daughter. Have a nice life." Should I write to my dad? Tell him that this was partially his fault? That if he'd been around, maybe I wouldn't have gotten into this mess in the first place? I don't even want to write to Mitch. And that surprises me. He has so occupied my thoughts and my actions these past three months. How can I so easily dismiss him now? Especially when he really seems to care about me. But does he? Or is he just worried about himself?

I go to my room for my notebook and a pen and bring them back to the table. As I open the notebook, a blank sheet of lined paper stares at me. I pick up the pen and write, "To Whom It May Concern." Now that's pretty personal. Then I write some stupid dribble about how this is all society's fault—echoing what Detective Sanders said earlier today. But I know it's stupid, and after a few sentences I tear the paper off, shred it up, and throw it away.

Get real, Miranda, I tell myself. *This is your*

mistake, and you're the one who needs to own up to it. Take the stupid pills and get this over with. Now!

But in this same instant I have this flashback. It's so real it seems it's happening right now. Only it's hazy too, like I can't quite see what's going on. Sort of like the night of the party—when this all happened in the first place. Anyway, I'm walking into the living room, carrying a plastic bowl that I just filled with cheese twists—talk about your empty calories—and I'm setting them on a table near the sofa. I see someone talking to Sammy, but I can only see this guy's back. It looks like he's telling Sammy a joke or maybe a secret, because their heads are bent toward each other, closer than in a normal conversation. The guy is a few inches shorter than Sammy, but he has about the same hair color. He's wearing a dark shirt with the tag sticking out of the neck. I can't make out who it is, exactly, but he's familiar. And I'm certain he's handing Sammy something.

I take in a deep breath, stand up, and go into the living room. I stare at the quiet room, with its furniture back in place, and wonder. Did I *really* see that happen? Or am I just imagining it now? I'm not sure. But it feels real to me. And it seems likely that if I can remember it, then someone else might as well. I go back to my notebook and start writing down names. Of course I don't know everyone who was there that night. But it's likely that the kids on this list would. I mean, I've never been to a party where someone doesn't know someone.

I've never seen a complete stranger walk in who isn't recognized by anyone. It just doesn't happen. I fold my list in half, but I know it's not complete. I didn't write down Mitch's name. I don't know why I still feel a need to protect him. Maybe it's because I'm certain he had nothing to do with Sammy's death. And because I know Mitch has the most to lose if his name appears on my list. So I leave him conspicuously missing.

I study the pills again, lined up like little white soldiers, all ready to do their work. I pick up the first one and put it in my mouth. It feels so small and harmless. I take a big swig of milk and swallow it. I take up the second pill and do the same. And then I wait a minute or two, holding the next pill in my hand. It's so small it reminds me of a seed, and I remember the first time I planted a garden with Nana. As we dropped the tiny seeds into the holes, she recited a Bible verse: "If you had faith as small as a mustard seed you could say to this mountain 'Move from here to there,' and it would move.

Back then those words made no sense to me, just as they make no sense to me now. But for some reason remembering them stops me, and I decide to drop this seed-sized pill back into the amber plastic bottle. Then, one by one, I drop the rest of them into the bottle—*plink-plink-plink*. I replace the child-protective cap, pick up my notebook and list, and walk to the bathroom. Even as I set the bottle back in its place on the shelf, right next to a white bottle of aspirin, I start to feel sleepy. I go to my room, collapse on my bed—and miraculously fall asleep. I can't even remember if I dream or not.

I don't wake up until 10:00 the next day. And amazingly, I feel better. Not great. But a little bit better.

I take a really long shower and dress, not carefully, and then walk to school. I try not to think about what I'm doing. I tell myself that I'm a robot, not a human. That I will simply go through the paces, attend class, get assignments, and then come home. That's it. I won't talk to anyone unless it's absolutely necessary.

For some strange reason I think I can do this.

It's 10 minutes before fifth period when I get
to school, and the halls are fairly vacant because
kids are still at lunch. As I walk to my AP history
class, it occurs to me that I could drop this class and
still graduate. In fact, I could easily drop three
classes and graduate. I only took these AP classes
because Ms. Whitman said it would increase my
chances of getting into a good college, possibly even
on a scholarship. Funny how that used to be terribly
important.

No one is in the classroom yet, and instead of
finding a front seat, I go for the back row, far corner, next to the window. I open my history book
and pretend to be reading, but my eyes don't focus
on the page. I remember how I used to do this on a
regular basis back in middle school—pretend to be

115

invisible—and it usually worked. No one ever wanted to sit next to me or converse or even look at me back when I was a nobody. I want to be a nobody again. It shouldn't be that hard.

Kids are coming in now. I feel them looking at me, and I hear their whispers. I try not to imagine what they're saying, thinking. But I can't help myself. "There's the girl who killed Sammy James." Or "Can you believe she has the guts to show her face here, after what she did?" Or "Poor Kyra . . . she used to think Miranda was her friend."

I turn and look out the window, out across the back field where Taylor and Rebecca and I used to jog together for soccer practice, laughing and joking, back when I was human. Dylan is in this class. I hear him greeting Jamie, a boyfriend I once had—back in another lifetime. I can feel the two of them scrutinizing me as they find their seats. They are both too nice to say anything mean, but I can guess what they're thinking. They were both close to Sammy. Even though they go to church and claim to be good Christians, I'm certain they must both hate me. How could they not? *I* hate me.

Mr. Harris is in the front now, droning on about the events that led up to the Civil War. I focus straight ahead with an expression that I hope conveys that I'm listening, but I don't process a single word from his thin tight lips. I'm only thinking that I should go tell Ms. Whitman that I want to drop these classes immediately. Better yet, I will write her a note. Then I won't need to have an actual conversation. I open my notebook and try to appear as if I'm taking notes. I write a sentence, then glance up front with feigned interest. Then I write a few more. Finally, my letter to Ms. Whitman is done. It looks very official, as if I'm giving my notice of resignation. And maybe that's what it is. I quit.

The clock says it's two minutes until the bell. I quietly slip my book and notebook into my backpack and wait like a sprinter on the blocks. Then, even before the bell is finished ringing, I am out of there. I go straight to the guidance counselors' office and drop my note on the receptionist's desk. The letter is neatly folded into thirds with Ms. Whitman's name clearly penned across the top. The receptionist is saying something to me, but I don't hear her. I am already out the door.

And then I head toward home. That wasn't too bad for my first day back at school. But it occurs to me that I have another piece of paper in my backpack. It is also folded into thirds and sealed in a white legal-sized envelope. I have tried to forget it, but it's almost as if this piece of paper is shouting at me. Demanding that I "do the right thing" and take it where it belongs. To the police station. And so I change my route and walk toward town. I am not eager to see the detective again, but perhaps I can do like I did at school—just leave it at the front desk. Yes, I decide, that's what I'll do. So I pick up my pace, eager to be done with this unpleasant task.

Yes, I know one name is conspicuously absent from my list. But I don't see how it could make any difference, really. Just because I have done something incredibly stupid doesn't mean I must inflict undue suffering onto Mitch. And the other names on the list have nothing to lose—compared to Mitch. Detective Sanders has already assured me that none of the kids present at the party can be charged with MIPs since they weren't arrested and breath-tested that night. They will only be subject to questioning, and probably only a few of them. And this is only to help the police establish and track the real problem, the drug trail. It seems ironic as I walk down Main Street—such an insignificant, quiet, and basically ho-hum little town—that we should have a "drug trail."

I enter City Hall more carefully today, afraid that I might run into the James family again. But they are nowhere in sight. I walk to the front desk and tell the woman the note is for Detective Sanders—the most words I've said today. Then, before anyone can stop me, I leave. I jog for home. I long for the privacy and security of my room.

I ignore the flashing red light on the answering machine and fix myself a bowl of Cheerios. This seems to be my mainstay for now. So far I've had three bowls in two days. I consider slicing a banana on top, but our bananas look old and spotty. The thought of something that mushy makes me feel that I might gag. I rinse my bowl, put it in the dishwasher, and look again at the answering machine. It says there are six messages, and I'm sure some of them are for me. Probably the newspaper reporter or police station. I know it will go better for me with Shelby if I delete them.

I play the messages. One is from a solicitor, three are from that moronic reporter, one is from Detective Sanders, reminding me of the list, and the last one is from the D.A.'s office. This one worries me the most, but I don't write down the number. Then I delete all but the solicitor so Shelby doesn't get too suspicious. I'm not sure what happens when you don't return the D.A.'s call, but I'm guessing I'll find out. I consider calling Detective Sanders and asking her. But I'm sure she'd tell me to call the D.A., and I don't want to do that. I don't want to talk to anyone.

I go to the bathroom and open the medicine cabinet. I take out the bottle of Ambien and gaze at it longingly—the same way I used to gaze at Nana's candy jar when I was little. I open the bottle and look at the little white pills. When I took just two yesterday, twice the recommended dosage, it wiped me out for nearly 16 hours. Sixteen blissful hours of nothingness. I don't even remember dreaming. But it's only three o'clock now. I suppose that's too soon to go to bed. Still, I shake out two pills and tuck them into my jeans pocket, certain that I'll need them later.

Then I go downstairs to Nana's old apartment. I'm not sure why. I just think it might be comforting. Since I still have my key, I unlock the door and tip-toe in. I don't know why I'm tiptoeing, but I am. Shelby hasn't had time to go through Nana's things yet. She says we'll have a big garage sale this summer—or, rather, *I* will have a big garage sale. But I cannot imagine selling Nana's things. Everything in here feels more familiar to me than the things in

Shelby's apartment upstairs. I guess that's because Shelby buys cheap things, uses them roughly, then replaces them with more cheap things after they fall apart. It's like she believes everything in life is replaceable.

I sit down on Nana's couch and rub my hand along its prickly surface. It's covered in chocolate-brown camel's hair that I used to think was quite ugly. But Nana defended her couch, telling me it would last forever. Over time I've grown somewhat attached to its bulky form and don't want to put it in the garage sale. Nana said her mother-in-law gave them this couch when they were first married, back in the late fifties, but even then it was old. Nana said she didn't like it at first and spent the best part of a week sewing up a pale yellow slipcover.

Nana was only 17 when she married my grandpa, but she said that wasn't so unusual back then. She and her husband lived in this house, back before it was sectioned off into apartments. Of course they always felt it was much too big for them with three stories, and they feared they'd never have children to fill it up. They didn't even have Shelby until Nana was in her late thirties. Back then that was considered way too old to be having babies. But Nana was glad.

The Bartlett family was pretty well off in those days. They had a good-sized farm just outside of town, as well as this "town house." My grandpa worked the farm but lived in town, since his parents were still happy to live out on the farm. Then one day my grandpa died while he was putting up corn.

Shelby was just a girl then, and the older Bartletts gave Nana the deed to the house, like it was some sort of consolation prize. My grandpa's younger brother inherited the farm. He lost it back in the eighties when farming was a bad business to be in. Nana kept the big old house and had it remodeled into four apartments. Two on the first floor, and two more on the second and third floors. Shelby chose to live on the top floor since it was the farthest one from her mother. But I don't really blame her because I think the view is nicer up there.

However, everything else is nicer down here. As I walk around the apartment and examine all the old pieces of furniture, it occurs to me that Shelby has no right to sell off all of Nana's things. It's the only family history we have, and for some reason it feels important to me right now. And yet what would I do with all this stuff? Especially if I were in jail. What use would it be to me if I were living in a completely furnished 10-by-10 cement cubicle?

I go into Nana's bedroom and lie down on her four-poster bed. Another piece that's been in the family a few generations. The metal springs in the old mattress squeak, and everything smells musty in here. It occurs to me that I should open the window and let some fresh spring air inside, but at the same time there's something about the musty odor that appeals to me. I guess it reminds me of death. And as I lie on the bed, I try to imagine myself dead. What a relief that would be. Okay, I know I chickened out last night. But that doesn't mean I can't do it today. And oddly, I find comfort in this thought.

I can kill myself today or tomorrow or even next week if I like. If I really decide to do this thing, no one can stop me. And, really, what are my other options? To continue like this? I don't think so. Living without being alive is so wrong. I'm sure Sammy would agree.

Oh, Sammy, where are you?

For now I settle for my two little pills. I take them one at a time, swallowing them without water. And then I wait for that white warm buzz to sweep me away. Ah, escape.

I awake to the sound of Shelby's voice. Shrill and irate, it's like a dull jagged knife cutting through my thick cocoon of slumber. I want her to go away.

"Get up, Miranda!" She's pulling on my arm now. "I mean it. I've had enough of this. *Get up!*"

I blink and sit up. It takes me a few seconds to figure out exactly where I am. Oh yeah, Nana's apartment. "What's wrong?" I try to focus my eyes on Shelby's face. But then I see she is glaring at me.

"*You!*" She folds her arms across her chest and taps her foot. "*You* are what's wrong. You're a mess."

"Yeah?" It's all I can think of to say.

"Last night I come home and think maybe you're just out with your friends or something, which is fine—you need to get out. But then it's after eleven and a school night, and you still aren't home. So I start getting worried. And for some reason—I have no idea what in the world made me come down here to look for you, probably all those times you pretended to run away from home when you were little—but anyway I decided to check down here."

"And so you found me." Feeling like a slug with a hangover, I crawl out of bed.

"Yeah, but then I can't wake you up. I shook you and yelled, but it's like you were drugged or something. I considered calling the hospital, but then you seemed to be breathing okay and everything." Now she leans over and peers into my eyes, like she's checking the size of my pupils. "Are you taking drugs, Miranda?"

For some reason I decide not to lie. "I just needed something to help me sleep, Shelby. I saw your bottle of Ambien in the—"

"You're taking my sleeping pills?"

"Only twice. I don't think I'll need to anymore." Now that's probably a lie.

She frowns. "Well, I guess I can understand it. You've been through a lot. But I, for one, am ready for this to be over with, Miranda. You need to get past this whole thing—the sooner the better."

I want to ask her exactly how I am supposed to do that—*get past this*—but I don't. I know she'd give me one of her Shelby answers. Like go out and get a pedicure, take a bubble bath, go shopping, or eat chocolate. But her cures don't work for me. Well, other than her sleeping pills.

"It's almost 7:30 right now, and I'm going to be

late for a sales meeting if I don't split. But as your mom, I am *insisting* that you go to school today, Miranda. You understand me? Hanging around here and feeling sorry for yourself isn't going to change a thing. Besides, you need to be with your friends right now. They're the ones who can help you get through this."

Without responding to her ludicrous suggestion about friends, I silently follow her through Nana's apartment. It's weird how Shelby sticks out like a foreign object in here with her magenta suit and high heels. So out of place. She waves as she heads out to her car, a shiny red Mustang that she swears she will *never* let me drive. Not that I care. I wouldn't want to be caught dead in that thing anyway. Well, maybe if I *were* actually dead. Local Girl Found Dead in Mother's Classic Mustang. That would be ironic, wouldn't it? It might give Shelby something special to remember me by every time she climbed into her precious car. For a moment I imagine myself slipping out late at night, tiptoeing over to the small detached garage that used to be a carriage house, silently closing the door, turning on the engine, and leaning my head back into the fleece that covers the driver's seat. It might be a peaceful way to go.

Feeling like a robot, I take a shower, then dress in the same clothes I wore yesterday. Old jeans and a T-shirt, topped with my gray hooded sweatshirt. I think this will be my new uniform. I eat my bowl of Cheerios and walk to school. I dread going to first period today. That's Mitch's class, and almost everyone I know is in that class. It used to be my favorite. Now I would switch it if I could.

I get there right as the last bell rings. Keeping my gaze down, I slip past 30 pairs of eyes, hoping for an empty seat in the back row. I feel like I can't breathe. But I take my seat and place my hands flat on the desk, as if to steady myself. I feel Mitch studying me as he begins to talk about a movie that's about to release, a retelling of Shakespeare's *Twelfth Night,* but I don't want to look up. I don't want to meet his gaze. Finally I allow my eyes a quick glimpse and he's looking directly at me. He smiles and, for an instant, I think everything might actually be okay. But then I see Kyra. Not in the front row where she would usually sit, but in the middle and off to the side—a place where she would never have willingly sat before. And she is looking at me too. But not with a smile. Oh, no. Kyra's eyes are an almost fiery color of green, yet they're as cold as ice. If a facial expression could kill, my worries would be over.

I look down fast, focusing my gaze on the cover of my shabby notebook. I take in a breath and wish I could vanish. I don't hear a single word that Mitch says after that, but the class seems to go on for days. Finally the bell rings. And yet I remain stuck in my chair. I am not going to stand up and walk through this room, taking the risk of seeing Kyra close-up. So I stay bent over my backpack, pretending to adjust a shoulder strap, as I wait for the classroom to empty.

"Miranda?"

Mitch is coming my way.

"You don't look too good."

"Uh-huh."

"I can see you're still hurting." He kneels now and looks into my face. "Were you able to get some rest?"

I nod.

"Did you take an Ambien?"

I nod again.

"Good. Sometimes we need a little help to get through the hard times."

"But I promised not to—anymore."

"You told your mother?"

"She found out."

"Oh."

I stand now, feeling uncomfortable. I head for the door.

"If you need something else—" he speaks quietly now—"to help you through this . . ." He glances over his shoulder to see kids starting to trickle in. "Come by the bike shop. I can help you." Then he pats me on the back and smiles. "You'll get through this, Miranda. Believe me, it'll get better in time."

I don't say anything as I leave the room. But I'm thinking he sounds a lot like Shelby. And for one weird moment I think the two of them might actually hit it off. That troubles me.

About midway through second period an office assistant brings in a note that turns out to be for me. *Great, all I need is a little more attention,* I think. It turns out to be from Ms. Whitman, who wants to see me in her office ASAP. I figure that means now, so I gather up my stuff, slip out the door, and head toward her office.

"I got your note," she announces as soon as I walk in.

"Uh-huh."

Then she looks up from her desk and stares at me as if she's just seeing me for the first time. "Miranda?" She removes her glasses. "Is that really you?"

I slump into a chair. "Guess so."

"I know how hard this must be for you," she says sadly, "losing a good friend like Sammy. I'm sure you're feeling pretty bad."

I swallow hard. For some reason I feel closer to crying when someone feels sorry for me. Fortunately that doesn't happen much.

"Have you seen a grief counselor yet?"

I shake my head.

"Oh, you need to do that." She picks up a phone. I hear her talking like she's doing some special scheduling, like she's trying to help some hopeless loser who I suppose must be me. "Andi's available now? Oh, that's perfect. Tell her to pencil in Miranda Sanchez. Oh, at least an hour, I think." She glances up at me. "Or longer. Tell her to leave it open-ended this morning."

Now I want to get out of here fast. Just run. But she's hanging up and smiling at me. "Okay, it's settled. You'll go see Andi immediately." She holds up my carefully constructed note, then tears it in two and tosses it into her wastebasket. "You are not allowed to make a choice that's this important while you're in the middle of grieving, Miranda. It would be wrong to hold you to this decision."

I stand up now, thinking, *I can make any decision I want. I can walk out of here and never come back if I want. Or I can go home and take all of Shelby's Ambien pills. I can go to bed and just sleep forever. No one can tell me what to do.*

But then I notice that Ms. Whitman is walking with me. She's still talking, but I haven't been listening. I feel her hand on my arm as if she's guiding me along. And as it turns out, she is.

"We set up the counselors in the cafeteria to start with because so many kids needed help those first two days. But it's slowed down a little today, and we only have one counselor in there now. We decided to move Andi Pierce into Mr. Canton's office since he's out the rest of this week anyway."

By now we're coming to an office, and a girl who appears to be about my age steps out the door and smiles. I don't recognize her, but I figure she must've been getting some counseling too. Maybe she was a friend of Sammy's I didn't know about. He had a lot of friends. I glance over my shoulder, hoping for one last escape, but this girl is coming straight toward me. Her hand is stretched out, like she wants to shake hands. I look curiously at Ms. Whitman, but she merely inclines her head toward this auburn-haired girl. "This is Andi Pierce."

"You must be Miranda," says the girl as she firmly shakes my hand.

I nod mutely.

"Well, come on in." She waves me into the small

office. "It ain't much, but it's all ours. For now anyway."

I walk in and stand dumbly by the door.

"Have a seat." Andi points to a chair set directly across from another chair with no desk to divide them. Then she sits down and sighs as she tucks one leg under the other. "I know this isn't easy."

I sit down too, but at the edge of my seat, as if I'm ready to bolt. I study her and wonder how old she is. Her hair is about the same length as mine but straight. She's wearing jeans and boots and a T-shirt, not any different from the way my friends dress. "You don't seem old enough—"

"Please!" Andi holds up both hands to stop me. "I've heard that line way too many times these past couple of days. Yes, you're right. I'm not that old. But I am 23, and I really do have my master's in counseling. And, yes, I'm still new at this. But I'm doing my best. Just give me a chance. Okay?"

"Whatever." I stick my right thumbnail into my mouth and bite down hard on what little cuticle remains there.

"You were pretty good friends with Sammy?"

I shrug.

"You mean you weren't?"

"Depends."

"On what?"

I shove my hands into my lap. "On how you define the word."

"The word?"

"Friend."

"How do you define it?"

I shrug again.

"I heard that Sammy died at your house."

I don't say anything now, just stare at my hands in my lap.

"How does that make you feel?"

I glance up. Andi has leaned slightly forward in her chair, studying me as if I'm some sort of lab specimen.

"How do you think it makes me feel?" I glare at her now.

"I'm sure you could be feeling a lot of things, Miranda. You might feel angry and sad and guilty—"

"And who cares?"

"You tell me." She folds her arms across her front and leans back.

Well, I am *not* going to make this any easier for her. After all, it's her stupid job to figure out what's wrong here, to do her grief-counseling thing. I plan on just sitting here like a dummy, to wait for her to perform some kind of miracle.

"I can tell you're hurting, Miranda."

I continue to glare at her.

"I can understand how you don't want to talk about this. It's not uncommon for someone who's lost someone to feel the way you do."

"And how's that?"

"Guilty."

I roll my eyes at her but restrain myself from saying, "Duh."

"And you actually have some good reasons to feel guilty. I understand that Sammy wasn't much

of a partyer, but that you and your friends encouraged him to loosen up and have some fun after
the play."

Why doesn't she tell me something I don't know?

"You hosted the party at your house, and when
Sammy was in trouble you didn't think anything
was really wrong. You didn't even want to call—"

"What good does this do?" I stand now, edging
toward the door. "The police already questioned
me. I confessed to everything. Why do you need
to—?"

"*You* need to, Miranda. *You* need to work through
your grief. Can't you see that you've bottled it all
up inside? You're like a powder keg that's about to
blow—"

"Fine." I reach for the doorknob. "Maybe I'll just
blow, then—"

"Miranda." She stands too, placing her hand
on the door. "What's it going to hurt to just talk
to me?"

"What's it going to help?"

"You might be surprised."

So I turn and really look at her. She does have
a kind expression, as if she really is concerned, but
it might be some trick she learned in college. And
I wonder why she should care about me. Probably
just because it's her job. She gets paid to listen to
losers like me.

"Do you plan on going to his funeral?" It feels
like she's changing the subject now or perhaps bait-
ing me with some new information.

But I just shrug.

"It's at 10:00 tomorrow morning, you know. They're letting kids out of school—the ones who want to go, anyway."

"Sounds like a good excuse to ditch school."

"Are you going?"

I imagine myself at Sammy's funeral, facing Kyra and her mom and dad, and I know I won't be able to do it. And yet the thought of not going—not saying a final good-bye to Sammy, my dearest friend—is a kick in the gut.

"Are you feeling torn, Miranda?"

I shrug again, but this time there's a slight convulsion in my chest. It's the closest I've been to tears so far. I'm not sure that I can keep a lid on this thing much longer. I look back at the chair. I consider sitting down and pouring out all the words and emotions that are writhing inside of me. What would happen if I removed the cork and just let it all go flying? Would this barely graduated counselor be able to catch all the pieces and then put them back together again? I doubt it. I seriously doubt it.

"Miranda." Andi places a hand on my shoulder. "I know you don't know me, and I'm sure you don't trust me. But you need to know that I feel like I know you. And I knew Sammy. We went to the same church, and I considered him my friend. I also happen to know that you and he were very close. What you're doing to yourself now is killing you. And you're hurting Sammy—"

"Stop!" I press my hands to my ears to mute her words. "I *know* I hurt Sammy—*I killed him*. Isn't that bad enough?" I reach for the doorknob again, and this time I open it and leave. I walk out of the school and decide I won't be coming back—ever.

14

No one seems to notice or care that I'm leaving the school. Instead of going straight home, I walk around town. I no longer worry about being seen by anyone. I am taking one last sentimental journey. And then, I think I will end this thing.

I walk by the grade school. I remember the first time I actually played with Kyra and Sammy together. It was the beginning of second grade, and Sammy was in my class. Kyra was in the other class since the school liked keeping the twins separated. I'm not sure why, since they always got along pretty well. But Sammy asked me to play with him at recess. At first this made his sister mad. She didn't like the idea of Sammy having another girl for his friend—like I was competition for her. But somehow Sammy convinced her that I was okay, and by the end of the week we all three became good friends. Sammy and I were both pretty quiet and shy, but Kyra was the social butterfly. She was always introducing one of her new little girlfriends into our threesome. As a result Sammy and I probably paired off even more. But I do remember feeling envious of the other girls that Kyra befriended over the years. They usually wore cute clothes and had the latest toy gadgets. I never really fit in with them. But because of Sammy I was included. As we grew older I became more competitive with sports. I loved playing football, basketball, soccer, and even baseball with the boys. And I had no problem keeping up with or even surpassing them during grade school. I guess that's when Sammy started calling me Randi. Like I was one of the guys. I loved that era.

I walk past the middle school now. Kids are starting to come out for lunch, gathering into little cliques as they sit on the grass. I can hear them teasing and taunting each other. Some in friendly jest, some not. During middle school I mostly felt lonely. And yet Sammy remained loyal to me during this complicated era. Even when I was gawky and clumsy, with beaverlike teeth and overgrown feet, Sammy was still my friend. The only place I ever felt comfortable during those years was playing sports or hanging with Sammy. The rest was simply an endurance test.

A test I thought I had passed in high school. But I was obviously wrong. I keep on walking now, eager to get away from the unhappy memories of middle school. And soon I find myself just a few blocks from Nana's nursing home. It seems only right that I pay her one last visit. Not that she'll notice or remember. But if this is to be my last "sentimental journey," it's fitting to see her.

Since they are still eating lunch, I am asked to wait. The receptionist explains that it can be disturbing to patients to visit them during mealtimes. So I sit in a vinyl-covered chair and pick up an old magazine. I absently turn pages as I wait.

Finally the receptionist tells me that lunchtime is over, and that I may now go to the dayroom. I find Nana sitting by the window again. So I go over and say hello.

Her eyes grow wide when she sees me. "Miranda?"

I am almost speechless as I grab a chair and scoot it right next to her. "You know me, Nana?"

She smiles. "Of course, dear."

"But you don't—"

She places her hand on mine. "I know, I know. My memory isn't so good anymore. But Dr. Porter is trying some new medications. He says I'll have good days mixed with bad. Today must be a good one."

"But you really remember me?" I am incredulous.

"Yes, my only granddaughter, Miranda Maria. Why wouldn't I remember you?"

"Oh, Nana." I wrap my fingers around her hand and, for the second time today, am seriously close to tears.

"Are you okay, Miranda?"

I'm unsure how much I should tell her. What if I pour out all my troubles to her and cause some sort of setback? I glance around the room, hoping to spy a nurse or someone who might be of help. "I need to go use the rest room, Nana," I say as I stand. "I'll be right back."

She nods and smiles.

I hurry out into the hallway and look until I see a uniformed nurse. "Helen Bartlett is my grand-mother," I quickly explain. "She has Alzheimer's, but for some reason is like her old self today."

"Yes," the nurse says. "Dr. Porter's been trying out some experimental medications. Your mother must've given her consent. It seems to help with some patients, but it's not terribly consistent."

"Well, I wasn't sure if I should say too much to her. Should I be careful not to upset her or any-thing? I just don't know . . ."

"I think you should treat her just like you used to. Who knows? It might even help her."

"You're sure?"

She laughs. "Nobody's really sure about anything when it comes to Alzheimer's. We just do the best we can."

So I hurry back to Nana, worrying that she might have regressed to her old forgetful self before I return. But she's still sitting there, smiling.

"Nana?" I venture.

"Did you find the bathroom?"

I take her hand again. "I am so glad to see you, Nana."

"Not as glad as I am to see you. I asked the doc-tor if I could go back home if this medication keeps working."

"What did he say?"

"He doesn't see why not. As long as I keep getting better."

"Can you remember everything?"

She shakes her head. "But I remember you. That's what's important, right?"

I peer into her eyes, still worried that I'm being tricked, or that suddenly it's all going to change. "I have missed you so much, Nana."

"I'm sorry."

"I even slept in your bed last night."

She frowns now. "You don't look well, Miranda. What's wrong?"

"Oh, Nana." I choke back a sob. "Sammy died."

"Oh, no. Not *our* Sammy." She puts her hand to her mouth. "Oh dear, how did it happen?"

I don't know how much to tell her. Despite what the nurse said, I am still afraid of upsetting her. "They think it was drugs, Nana."

She closes her eyes and moans. "Oh, poor Sammy." Then she opens her eyes and looks at me. "But Sammy wasn't like that, was he, Miranda? He wasn't one of those kids who takes drugs—"

"No, they think it was an accident or something. He never used drugs before. He didn't even drink. They think someone might've slipped him something." Okay, this is pretty speculative, but I don't know how else to tell her. I sure hope she doesn't read the newspapers.

"Oh dear." She sighs deeply now, and her face looks as if this bad news has aged her by about 20 years. I seriously regret telling her.

"I'm sorry, Nana," I begin. "I shouldn't have told you about—"

"Nonsense, Miranda. You always told me everything. And, as I recall, Sammy was a strong Christian boy. He went to church regularly and his faith was firm. So we know he's safe with God now, don't we?"

I try to nod but feel it's not convincing.

Now she searches my eyes. "But how are *you* doing, dear?"

"Not so well."

"It's very sad, dear. Very sad to lose someone you love."

"I don't really have anyone to talk to about it, either."

"What about your mother?"

"You know how Shelby can be . . . she just thinks I should get on with my life. But it's not that easy."

"How about Kyra?"

"She's so devastated."

"Yes, I see. Well, it's good that you came to me. Do you know how I got over losing your grandfather?"

I shake my head.

"I learned how to lean on God. Your grandfather had always been a strong Christian man, and naturally I went to church with him. But I never had any real faith of my own. When he died . . . well, I was utterly lost and brokenhearted. And I had a little girl to raise all by myself. Goodness, I was a complete mess."

"What did you do?"

"I started reading your grandfather's old Bible. He'd left a bookmark in it, right in the middle of the New Testament. So I started reading there. And before long I started to pray too. Just short little prayers to start out with. Finally, one Sunday about a month after losing your grandfather, I took Shelby to church as usual. But when the pastor gave a call to come forward and give your heart to God, why, I just took Shelby's little hand and walked right up there and did it."

"Gave your heart to God?"

"That's right," she replies. "And sometimes when I can't remember a single thing, I can still remember how to pray. And I can remember things I've read in the Bible." She smiles. "That reminds me, Miranda. Will you bring me my old Bible the next time you come to visit?"

"Sure. I just saw it by your bed."

She smiles even more now. "You really slept in my old bed?"

"I felt better down there."

Her eyes light up. "Why don't you stay down there, Miranda? Take care of things for me until I get better?"

"Really?" Then I remember that Shelby has guardianship over Nana. "But Shelby might not like that."

"You tell Shelby to come over here and talk to me about it then."

"Has she been by?"

"Not that I remember." Nana winks. "But that doesn't mean anything much."

Still, I doubt that Shelby's visited. "I'll tell her that you're better. I'll tell her to come see you."

Now Nana grabs me by both hands. "And just in case, Miranda—in case I go back to being old crazy and forgetful Nana—I want you to know how much I love you, dear. And how much God loves you. Oh, I know losing Sammy is terribly hard on you. Why you two were like—" Then she taps a finger on her head as if she can't remember what she wanted to say. "Well, *you know*. But you've got to understand that only God can get you through something like this. Do you understand that, Miranda?"

I pretend I do understand as I swallow against the hard lump that's growing in my throat.

"You've got to lean on God now, Miranda." Nana peers into my eyes as if she's peering into my soul. "Just like I learned to do. And no matter how hopeless you feel, you can't give up."

"I'll try, Nana."

She squeezes my hands. "I'll be praying for you, dear."

I glance up at the clock. I haven't really been here that long, but I'm afraid if I stay any longer I'll start to cry and spill the whole horrible story to Nana. I know it will only upset her, even more than I already have. So I stand. "I better get going now."

"Come back, Miranda. Come visit me again."

I lean over and kiss her cheek. "I will, Nana." I'm not sure if it's true or not. I'm not sure what I'm doing, who I am, or even where I'm going when I leave here. All I know is that I don't want to hurt her.

I leave and start walking toward home. Earlier today I felt certain that I would not be alive by the end of this day. Now I am not so sure. I go home and open the medicine cabinet only to find that Shelby has removed all her prescriptions. She obviously doesn't trust me. Instead I go and open the box of Cheerios, but there is only enough for half a bowl. I empty the box, pour on milk, and eat the cereal standing up. Then I go get my bike and ride around town for a while. Finally I stop on the bridge that crosses over Alder River and park my bike. I stare down into the fast-moving water and wonder if the bridge is high enough to actually kill a person stupid enough to jump from it. With my luck I'd survive with multiple injuries. Local Girl Fouls Suicide Attempt from the Alder Bridge. Why take chances?

I think about Mitch's offer this morning. He says he has something to help me get through this. So I ride my bike over to the shop. If I hurry I can get there just about the time he normally shows up after school, but early enough that the biker crowd won't have arrived yet. I really don't want to see my old biking buddies today.

Mitch is just parking his Porsche in back when I breathlessly pull up. I gasp out his name as my wheels grind to a stop in the gravel.

"Miranda." He smiles as he locks his doors. "Are you going to ride with us today?"

"No."

He unlocks the back door and waits for me to go in.

"I need something, Mitch."

He turns on the lights. "Something to help you get through this?"

"Yes." I'm not even sure what I expect him to do. But somehow I believe he can do something.

He takes off his jacket, sits down on a stool, and scratches his chin as if he's thinking. "What did you have in mind?"

"I don't know." I bite into my lip. "Shelby took all of her pills out of the medicine cabinet. I guess I just need something to help me sleep."

"That's simple," he says. "I can give you a few pills."

"A few?"

He eyes me more closely now. "How many do you need?"

I look down at the floor.

"Miranda?"

I turn away. "I guess I should go."

He puts his hand on my shoulder. "Wait."

I turn back to see his face. He seems concerned. Then suddenly I find myself pleading, "Mitch, I can't take it anymore. The police questioning, the newspaper reporter, that counselor chick at school. I just want out of this . . . this—"

"This what?"

"This everything."

"So if I gave you a bottle of sleeping pills, what would you do? Take the whole thing and call it a day?"

I shrug.

"Can't you see that you're really depressed, Miranda?"

I'm angry with him now. "Yeah, maybe I should go see a shrink."

"Maybe."

I start for the door. Why was I duped into thinking he wanted to help me? I feel betrayed for even trusting him. Why am I so stupid?

"Wait, Miranda."

"Forget it."

"No, I think I know what you need."

I stop and, for a minute, wonder why everyone but me seems to know what I need. All I think I really need is a way to escape all of this. To just check out—once and for all.

"Look, I know you're really down about Sammy. I wouldn't be surprised if you're considering the possibility of joining him, right?"

I give Mitch my blankest expression. Pure nothingness.

"Maybe you do need something to help you sleep at night. That's not so surprising. But I think you need something to help you out of this blue funk as well. If you trust me with this, I'll try to help you. Okay?"

My nonanswer is an answer.

"But first I need you to tell me why you didn't call Paul."

"Who?"

"The attorney."

I sigh. "I don't want a lawyer."

"But what about the police? The possibility of charges?"

"What about it?"

"You don't care?"

"Why should I?"

He seems to consider this. "Well, maybe you shouldn't. Like I said, it's all probably going to blow over. Did they ask about me again?"

Tired of this line of questioning, I head for the door again. Why did I imagine he would help me anyway? I hear him opening and closing a cabinet, but I keep on going. I am out of here.

But he follows me outside. "Wait, Miranda!"

I turn and start to tell him to forget it, but he's beside me now.

"Give me your hand, Miranda."

"Huh?"

He takes my hand and drops something into my palm. "The blue ones are to help you sleep, and the yellow ones are to help you get going in the morning." He glances over his shoulder. "I'm only giving you enough for two days. We'll talk later."

15

I think about Nana as I pedal home. I think about how she would feel if I kill myself right after her medication started working. It would probably send her straight down memory-loss lane again. So for Nana's sake I decide not to kill myself today. I'm not sure about tomorrow, though. But I do like what Nana said about me living in her apartment until she comes home. I decide to take her up on this offer and spend the rest of the afternoon moving all of my stuff down there. I don't put it away but simply heap it all over the place until Nana's neat little apartment looks like a hurricane hit. Then I explore her kitchen cupboards and find that she still has some food staples here. If I worked at it, I could probably even survive here for a while.

Unfortunately she has no Cheerios. But then, neither does Shelby now.

I make myself a cup of black tea and go sit by the window that overlooks the backyard. I wait for Shelby to come home and find out what I have done. I'm not sure how she'll react, but I expect it won't be good. Although it's a perfectly sunny afternoon, I sit here, waiting for the storm.

It's just before six when I hear her banging on the door. I have taken both keys so she can't just unlock the door and let herself in. I slowly walk to the door, preparing myself for the battle.

"What on earth are you doing?" she demands as I open the door.

I'm slightly relieved to see that she's changed into her aerobic workout clothes. Today it's the lavender-and-pink getup. At least she won't be here long. "I went to see Nana today."

"So?" She eyes me as if I'm the one who has lost my mind. Like it's only a matter of time before she'll be taking me over to the nursing home and booking me a room right next to Nana's.

"Nana *knew* me."

Shelby rolls her eyes. "Well, she does that sometimes, you know. She gets lucky with her guessing."

"No, that's not it. The doctor has her on some new experimental medication that's really working. Nana and I talked for a long time. I told her about Sammy, and she told me about my grandpa and everything."

Shelby doesn't look entirely pleased. "Are you kidding?"

"No," I say. "I told her that I spent the night here last night. She said she'd like me to stay here until she can come home."

"She really said that?"

"Yeah. She wants you to come visit her so she can tell you all this herself."

"You're serious?"

"Really, Shelby. She was like her old self."

Then I notice what might be a trace of hope in Shelby's eyes. For a split second I wonder if my mother is as bad as I usually assume. But then she swears. "Well, this really throws a wrench in the works now, doesn't it?"

"Huh?"

"Just when I thought I could sell this place and get out of here." She pushes a loose strand of bangs off her forehead. "I've already been looking into those new condos over on Fairway Drive. I hear they might even put in a golf course in a few years."

"But what if Nana gets better and wants to come home?"

Shelby frowns. "It's not like I don't want Mom to get better, Miranda. It's just that you never know about these experimental drugs. They told me the drug could have some bad side effects. Who knows what she'll be like tomorrow? She might be growing hair and fangs and howling at the moon."

Yeah, sure, I think. *That sounds more like you, Shelby!* But I keep my mouth shut and stare at the floor.

"Well, I guess it doesn't hurt anything for you to stay down here." She brightens now. "In fact, I don't know why I didn't think of this sooner. Now I can use your room for my home office."

So just like that I am moved out and on my own. Back in the old days, if something this important had happened, I would've immediately called Kyra and invited her over to celebrate with me. Or if Kyra was busy, Sammy. But not anymore. Those days are gone.

I remember the pills in my sweatshirt pocket and feel a small wave of relief. It's like those pills are buying me time somehow. Why that is remains a mystery to me, but somehow I make myself believe it's true.

Not long after Shelby leaves I hear this quiet *tap-tap* on the door. I peer out the tiny peephole to see old Mr. Campton standing there with a puzzled expression on his face. I open the door and try to make my face appear happy to see him.

"Hello, Mr. Campton." I speak in a loud voice because I know he's a little hard-of-hearing.

"Why, Miranda, I thought I saw you carrying a bunch of stuff down here today. When I saw your mother leave just now, I thought that perhaps Mrs. Bartlett had come back home."

"No," I say sadly. "But I saw her today, and she was doing a lot better. She said I could live down here for now. And hopefully, if she keeps getting better, she'll get to come home before too long."

I'm not sure if he really got all that or not, since he adjusts his hearing aid, but he smiles. "Well, wouldn't that be nice. I've missed her. We used to sit out back and visit on a regular basis. It's been mighty lonely without her."

"Yes. I can imagine," I say.

"That old feral cat is back again. I know your mother doesn't like me feeding her, but I think she's got some kittens with her this time."

"Really?" I try to appear interested, but I really just want to close the door.

"Yes. I think she's got them tucked away behind that old juniper shrub that's so overgrown in the corner." He has a sheepish expression now. "I know I shouldn't feed her, but it's awful hard not to, seeing she's a mother and all."

I try to force the corners of my lips up. "I think it's probably okay. Seeing she's a mother and all."

"You won't tell your mother now, will you?"

I make a zipper motion over my mouth. "My lips are sealed, Mr. Campton."

He grins. "Maybe you can come out and see them. The kittens, I mean. You never know—they might be real cute."

I slowly close the door as I speak. "Yes, I'll come see them sometime."

I go back into the apartment and sit down at Nana's old dining table. Unlike Shelby's, this one is made of solid wood. Maple, I think Nana said. I can't even begin to remember how many meals I've eaten down here. Just the thought almost makes me hungry. Almost.

I root through her cupboards, realizing I'd have to be really hungry to eat things like canned beets or green beans. But I finally spot a can of peaches, and somehow the idea of the sun-colored fruit appeals to me. I eat most of them and put the

remains in the fridge, which is still running. Probably because Shelby didn't want to clean it out.
I peek in the freezer and find several things that might still be good, as well as what appears to be a cup of coffee that's frozen rock-hard. Nana must've gotten confused.

It surprises me to realize that Nana's been gone less than three months. Of course, Sammy's only been gone about four days and it feels like another lifetime. I suddenly remember what Andi the counselor said about Sammy's funeral being tomorrow morning. Like she was setting me up. She said it was at 10:00, and I'm assuming it will be at the Jameses' church. As much as I wish I could go, I know I cannot show my face there. It would be so wrong.

I feel in my pocket again for the pills that Mitch gave me. Now I'm pretending they're like Jack's magic beans. I imagine myself planting them and watching as they grow into a giant beanstalk, and up, up, up I will climb. And I will be taken far, far away from this hopeless little life.

Finally, it's only 8:00, but I decide to take the blue pill (if I remember correctly it's the one to help me sleep). I am curious to find out if it will actually put me to sleep or not. He only gave me two of each pill, and since he said they are "two days' worth," I figure that means I only get to take one at a time. However, I toy with the idea of taking the second blue pill if the first one lets me down.

Amazingly, I do not wake up until the following morning. It seems that Mitch's pills are even better than Shelby's. I begin to wonder where he got them and whether or not he can get me some more. It's now 7:00, according to Nana's clock radio.

I just had this frighteningly vivid dream. I sit in bed for a few minutes, trying to sort it all out. The dream was about Nana, only it was so real it felt like it was me. She was going to her husband's funeral and getting lost and then crying a lot.

As I get out of bed and look around Nana's bedroom, now cluttered with my things, I wonder if I really had this dream. Or was it actually some sort of flashback or hallucination from being in Nana's room? Whatever it is makes no sense to me, and it only makes me feel sadder. But at the same time I feel envious of the Nana in my dream for her ability to cry. I've forgotten how.

I take a shower and, wanting to be closer to Nana, I even powder myself with her French Violet talcum powder until I smell like an old woman. I try not to see my body in the fogged mirror. But I can see that it's long and gangly and slightly ashen in color. It's odd because, even though I'm half Hispanic and can carry off a pretty spectacular tan in summer, my natural coloring can turn pale and sallow, especially if I'm sick. And I know that I look sick now. But what does it matter?

I wrap myself in Nana's old bathrobe, the aqua chenille one that she's had forever. I wonder why Shelby didn't pack it with her things for the nursing home, but then Shelby never liked this bathrobe. She sent the pink satin one instead. *Poor Nana,* I think, *trying to feel warm and snug in such a flimsy*

miranda's story

excuse of a bathrobe. I make a mental note to put this one in my backpack and take it to her the next time I visit, along with her Bible. Maybe I'll do that today.

As I go back into Nana's bedroom, I am still haunted by my weird dream. It felt so real. And then as I consider dressing for school I am reminded that today is Sammy's funeral. Perhaps that's why I had the dream. But unlike Nana, I will be forced into exile for I know I am not welcome there. This thought falls down on me like a heavy blanket of gloom. I feel I will suffocate beneath it. I wonder if I can make it through another day—or why I should even try. Then I hear Nana's hopeful voice, begging me to come back and visit her again.

I remember the yellow pills that Mitch gave me— the ones to help me make it through the day. I wonder if these will work as well as the blue ones. What can it hurt? I go to the kitchen and slowly fill a glass with tap water. I put the yellow pill on my tongue, take a drink, then swallow. Unsure what to do next, I sit down on the camel-hair sofa and wait. At first I feel nothing. But then, slowly at first, then faster, a warm rush sweeps over me, almost like an electrical buzz. For the first time in days I actually feel alive again. Or something that faintly resembles alive. It's hard to describe really. But definitely different than before. After a few minutes I hear Shelby coming down the stairs and I decide to reassure her that I'm still here. I stick my head out the door and wave. I even tell her to have a nice day at work. She looks at me as if I'm slightly deranged. Maybe I am.

Then I walk around Nana's apartment, as if I'm testing out this new feeling. Will it go as quickly as it came? But to my surprise I suddenly feel as if I can face this day. Maybe even conquer it. I consider getting dressed and going to school, but then I remember the funeral. Despite my chemical-induced feeling of near euphoria, I'm still not completely sure I can face that. I go into the bedroom and look at myself in the mirror. Wearing Nana's frumpy bathrobe, I suddenly imagine myself as an old woman. *Now if I were an old woman, like Nana, I could attend Sammy's funeral without being noticed at all. That's it—I can wear a disguise!*

I walk to Nana's closet and poke around for something to wear. Finally I come up with an outfit that appears to be from the '50s. It's dark gray, about the color of pencil lead, and has a jacket to go with it. Amazingly these pieces both fit, although the skirt is on the short side, for an old lady anyway. It's just below my knee and I'm sure it's meant to be mid-calf. It's quite frumpy and horrid-looking, and I manage to find a hat that almost appears to go with it. The hat is charcoal-colored velvet with a netted veil that comes down clear below my nose. I powder my hair until it appears to be gray, then pull it back into a tight bun. I securely pin on the hat and pull down the veil. With the help of some pasty makeup and some penciled-in wrinkles that I learned how to do when we put on the play, I think I am quite convincing. The only thing missing is

stockings and shoes. Naturally, Nana's don't fit. So
I dig through my things until I finally find an old
pair of panty hose and the black flat pumps that I
used to wear back when I was still in orchestra and
we had our seasonal concerts where I looked—oh,
so much—like a geek as I played on my clarinet. Of
course, Sammy never thought so as he sat beside
me playing his sax. But that was so long ago.

Finally I examine myself in the full-length mirror
that hangs on her closet door and realize that I look
hideous. Anyone could see through this pitiful disguise. What was I thinking? I wipe off the makeup
and quickly replace Nana's clothes with my usual
jeans and sweatshirt. Then I glance desperately
around the messy room. I return to Nana's closet
and peer back in the corner, where I'd noticed a
few items of men's clothing earlier. I assume these
belonged to my grandfather. I take out the long tan
raincoat that looks like it could swallow a person
whole. I shake the dust from the shoulders, then slip
it on. It goes nearly to my ankles. Then I notice a
black felt hat, the kind men wear in old movies. I
shake the dust from it too and place it on my head.
I peer in the mirror again. Not bad, really. I stuff
my hair inside the hat and put on a pair of dark
glasses. Now this might work.

The church is already full when I arrive. Friends
of Sammy's are acting as ushers. When Jamie
Cantrell sees me, he quickly finds a folding chair
and sets it at the end of an aisle toward the back.

"Here you go, sir," he says in a polite voice. Have
I fooled him, the guy I actually dated last winter?

Despite the whole sadness of this situation, this makes me want to laugh. But I manage to contain myself, pretending to cough instead. I slowly ease myself into the chair and hunch forward, holding my head down, just in case anyone is looking my way. But I know they're not. It's as if I'm invisible. The invisible man. I toy with wearing this disguise for the next several years. Or at least until school is out. But then again, it might not work at Macon High. An old-man student would probably be a little suspicious there.

I look around the crowded church. So many kids from school. So many other people—some familiar, some not. All here to say good-bye to Sammy. It is so wrong.

Then my eyes fall upon the casket that sits like a prop at the front of the church. At first I almost don't notice it because flowers are everywhere. A sea of carnations and roses and chrysanthemums. But there it sits, a painful reminder of the reason I'm here. The casket shines like a polished car. It's a smoky blue, not a color Sammy would like. He never went for the somber colors. He liked colors that were bright and lively. But now he's dead.

Oh, Sammy, where are you?

You're not in that box with the polished chrome handles, surrounded by hundreds of hothouse blooms that probably smell like the girls' locker room—a bad mix of deodorant, perfume, and sweat. You're not stretched out lifelessly on some white satin or velvet. Not wearing some awful suit that you never would've actually worn in real life. Unless you were playing

your saxophone at one of our horrible concerts. I
look down at my old concert shoes and remember
when Sammy was alive.

I don't hear too much of what is said in the
funeral. All I can do is stare at the casket and tell
myself that Sammy is not in it. Even when friends
from school step up to the podium and share memories, I barely listen. I see the tears on Dylan's face,
shining in the bright overhead lights, as he talks
about something that Sammy once told him. I watch
as Taylor and Rebecca take turns talking about
Sammy, but their words are fuzzy and blurry. It's as
if I'm here . . . but not. I'm not sure if it's the chemi-
cals running through my body or that I'm simply
losing my mind. Maybe it's both. Perhaps it doesn't
matter.

Finally, more music is played, more prayers are
said, and people begin filing up past the casket.
First it's Mr. and Mrs. James, with Kyra in the middle. They are holding on to each other, as if they
are supporting one another. I wonder what it would
feel like to belong to something like that—a real
family—where people hold on to you and keep you
from falling.

I bow my head and pretend to pray like an old
man might do. I'm not sure how much time has
passed, but finally I feel a nudge on my arm. It's
Jamie again. For a fearful second I think he has
recognized me. But he is simply gesturing toward
the front.

"Would you like to go up, sir?"

I slowly stand, as if my bones are aching. And

I think they are. Then, with my shoulders stooped and head bowed, I slowly make my way to the front, shuffling slightly. Only a few people remain, including Mr. Clean, our janitor from school, and a couple of kids I barely recognize. Sammy was friends with everyone.

I politely wait while they stand by the casket. I remain in character. But then suddenly—like a cold bucket of water poured over my head—I realize exactly what I am doing. It's like I've been living out this weird dream, but now I'm fully awake and I realize that Miranda Maria Sanchez has dressed up like an old man to come to her best friend's funeral. It's so totally bizarre. And, as Sammy would say, "Wrong, in so many ways." I feel my head starting to swim and know I should turn around and leave this place before something really horrible happens. What if I pass out, and everyone sees that it's really me? Local Murderer Disguised As Old Man Crashes Sammy James' Funeral.

But in this same moment, I know I must go and look in the casket for myself. I honestly believe there's this possibility that Sammy may not be in there at all. This whole thing could be a giant hoax. And those serious-looking flowers and that smoky-blue casket . . . well, it's so unlike him.

I tell myself it's all a big mistake as I step forward. That someone else died that night. There was a mistake at the hospital, and Sammy is lying in a bed somewhere on the fourth floor of the hospital—just waiting for his family to come and take him home. And so, as the last girl steps away from the casket, tears streaming down her red blotchy face, I walk over and, taking a deep breath, look down.

16

Sammy appears to be asleep. I reach in and touch his cheek, thinking I'll awaken him, tell him it's time to get up. Say, "Hey, let's go do something." But his cheek is cold. Just like that night. It really did happen. Sammy really did die.

I stand there just looking at him and know that *I* caused this. That Sammy James, the friend I love, is dead because of me. I take my hand back and place it over my mouth. I feel a sob—huge and uncontrollable—rising up in me like a tidal wave. Like it's going to choke me.

"I'm sorry, Sammy," I whisper. "So sorry." I think my heart is breaking now—or perhaps I am having a heart attack. Can an 18-year-old have a heart attack? The pain in my chest is unbearable, like fiery coals. And my head throbs, like it might

explode. I step away and it seems the hideous flowers, the shiny casket, even Sammy's sweet face are
all spinning away from me. I reach out for something to grasp, something I can hang on to, but
there is only the air. And then I feel myself tumble
into darkness. . . .

When I come to, I'm partially sitting, partially
sprawling across a hard wooden bench. Actually it's
a church pew. It takes me a moment to remember
where I am, what happened. I look down to see my
grandfather's raincoat and suddenly feel mortally
embarrassed about my stupid disguise. What in the
world was I thinking? What have I done?

"You okay, Miranda?"

I peer up from under the big black felt hat to see
Jamie looking down on me. His eyes seem so sad.

"Does anyone else know?" I whisper.

"I don't think so," he says quietly.

"What happened?"

"I think you were about to faint. I caught you
and helped you over here."

I glance over my shoulder. "I am such a moron."

He sits down beside me. "You do look pretty
weird in that getup." He's almost smiling now.

"I know. I'm such a complete imbecile, but I
didn't want to miss his funeral. And I knew nobody
wanted me here—"

"Sammy wanted you here, Miranda."

"I killed Sammy, Jamie. Everyone knows it."

Jamie reaches over now and takes my hand. He
gives it a firm squeeze, like he's trying to get my

attention. "That's not true. All you did was have a party—"

"A stupid party. A party that never should've happened," I say bitterly.

"No one disagrees with you there," he says. "But you are no more to blame for Sammy's death than I am . . . or Dylan or Kyra, for that matter."

I roll my eyes. "You three would be the last ones to blame."

Jamie glances over to the casket now, and tears fill his eyes. "Don't be so sure about that, Miranda."

"Everything okay up there?" a voice calls from the rear of the church. It sounds like Dylan.

"Yes," Jamie calls back. "This, uh, gentleman just got a little light-headed is all."

"Need any help?" Another voice.

"No, he's fine now."

I sit up. "I better go." I peer around the pulpit area, purposely avoiding the front section where the casket and flowers are placed. "Is there an exit up here?"

"I'll walk you to it."

I stand, and Jamie takes my arm as if he's escorting a feeble old man. "How did you know it was me, Jamie?" I ask when we reach the door.

"Your shoes."

I sigh.

"Most old guys don't wear girl's shoes, Randi."

I shiver, surprised that Jamie's called me by the same name that Sammy always used. "Thanks," I mumble. "For the help, I mean."

"We should talk sometime," he says as he opens the door.

The sunlight is so bright that I'm momentarily blinded. "Yeah, I guess."

"I'm not just saying that, Miranda. There are a few things you need to hear. About Sammy, I mean."

"Uh-huh." My chest is still hurting, and I'm not sure how much more I can take right now. "I better get out of here, Jamie."

"Yeah, I gotta get back too. I'm a pallbearer, you know. Never expected to do something like this— for a friend, I mean."

I turn back toward Jamie. "You were a *really* good friend to Sammy, Jamie. He always spoke so well of you. Even when you and I were going out . . . well, you know, even *then* Sammy said you were the best. That's something."

He presses his lips together. "Yeah, that is."

"See ya," I say as I turn away.

"Take it easy, Randi."

I walk slowly through the back parking lot, shoulders hunched, head down, continuing my old-man act that's surprisingly comfortable. The lot is still fairly full of cars, although some people are starting to leave now, gathered into small groups. Their heads are bent toward each other, offering comfort the way a community does when you belong to it. I try to avoid looking anyone in the eye, afraid that they, like Jamie, might recognize me. But no one seems to even see me. I am still invisible, and I'm grateful.

Back at Nana's apartment, I remove my detestable disguise and throw it onto the floor. Then, feeling guilty about abusing my grandfather's old clothes, I pick them up, shake them off, and put them back in the corner of Nana's closet. I close the door and wonder if I should be locked up, either in prison or the mental ward. I'm not sure that it matters which.

I realize that I haven't eaten anything since the canned peaches yesterday and wonder if that's not part of my problem. And strangely enough—maybe it's because of that yellow pill—I do feel slightly hungry. But not for beans and beets. I go up to Shelby's apartment and make myself a peanut-butter sandwich, washing it down with a glass of milk. And I think perhaps I might be able to drag myself to school for my afternoon classes.

Somehow I make it through the entire afternoon without having an actual conversation or even running away. That's probably because so many kids are still absent and teachers are acting pretty laid-back. It's like a nonday. And I feel like a nonperson. Or a zombie. Alive on the outside, but dead underneath. I wish I were with Sammy right now. I imagine myself lying next to him in that casket. I try to remember what the lining was like—kind of a pale blue velvet if my memory is right. It looked soft and cushy, anyway. Comfortable. I imagine the lid down, clamped tightly into place. It would be dark and quiet in there. I think I could be happy there. If I knew what happy was, that is.

As I walk home from school, I decide that I'll go visit Sammy's grave later on today. I'm fairly sure he must be buried up at Macon Memorial. I'll ride my bike up there later, maybe around the dinner hour. When I can be fairly sure that no one else will be there since most normal people will be sitting with their families, having dinner, and talking about the sad event of the day. Maybe I can talk to Sammy up there, clear some things up.

I notice that some flowers are blooming in Nana's backyard. She used to love to grow things, and her tulips, hyacinths, and daffodils are already blooming profusely. I decide to pick some and make a bouquet for Sammy. Just when I think it looks about perfect, I hear Mr. Campton shuffling out.

"Hello there, young lady," he calls in a cheerful voice.

"Hello," I answer with what I hope doesn't sound like encouragement.

"You enjoying our fine spring weather?"

I nod.

He smiles at my canning jar that's filled with flowers. "That's a mighty pretty bouquet you got there, Miranda. You taking those over to your grandmother?"

I consider lying and saying yes. But somehow it feels wrong to deceive someone as old and nice as Mr. Campton. "No, these are for a friend—he, uh, died. I wanted to take them to his grave."

Mr. Campton frowns. "Oh, that's right. That young Samuel fellow. I don't get the paper anymore. My eyes aren't sharp enough to read that fine print. But I heard about it at the grocery store the other day. He was a friend of yours, wasn't he?"

Relieved that Mr. Campton hasn't read the paper, I say, "Yeah. A good friend."

He eases himself down into one of the old wooden lounge chairs and sighs. "You care to join me? Shoot the breeze for a while?"

I see the empty chair beside him, the one that Nana used to sit in, and decide it can't hurt anything. So I set my jar of flowers on the small table between us and sit down.

"You feeling bad about your friend, Miranda?"

I notice that his face is creased with concern. "Yeah. I guess I am. His funeral was today."

"It's always the saddest thing when young folks die. My oldest boy, Bill Junior, died in Vietnam back in 1966. Hardest trial I ever had to endure." He winces, as if the memory still hurts him. "Never seems right to outlive your own children."

"I'd give anything to have Sammy back," I say.

"How are Sammy's folks doing?"

"I—uh—I don't really know."

"But weren't you good friends with those kids? What was his sister's name again? Kiwi . . . or something like that?"

"Kyra. I haven't really talked to her, well, since it happened."

"How'd the boy die? Wasn't it an accident or something?"

I lift my eyes to the window above us, the third floor, and try not to remember that night. "Yeah, kind of a freak accident."

"Well, as hard as it is to accept, especially when

it comes to what seems like an untimely death, I do believe that God knows what he's doing."

"Really?" I lean over and study Mr. Campton's face. "Is that how you felt when your son died?"

"No, not at the time. At the time I was angry and upset." He smacks his knee for emphasis. "Why, I thought God was the worst, spiteful, mean, nasty, malicious being ever. I was so mad at God that I quit going to church for about 10 years."

"What happened to change things?"

"My wife died."

"Oh."

"Clara was a jewel of a woman, and despite my horrible views on God and life in general, she managed to maintain her faith and happy spirit throughout everything. She kept right on going to church and taking care of our family. We had two other teenagers still in high school back then. She said that's the way young Billy would've wanted it. He'd always been involved in church and whatnot."

"How did your wife die?"

"Breast cancer."

"I'm sorry."

"She hung on for three long years. It was during that time that she helped me find my way back to God. She always used to say that God was the blessed controller of all things. And I've come to accept that as true."

"But it's still hard."

"Oh yes," he says slowly. "Losing someone is always hard. But I plan to meet up with both of them again on the other side." He smiles up at the sky. "I'm thinking it won't be too long, either."

I sigh and think it's one thing to lose someone you love, but something entirely different to be the reason that person is gone. I'm sure Mr. Campton wouldn't understand how I feel.

"I can't wait to grab my boy up in my arms," Mr. Campton continues, as if he's talking to himself now. "I've told him over and over how sorry I am. But I reckon I won't be completely happy until I see him face-to-face and know for a fact that he's forgiven me."

"Forgiven you?"

"Oh yes. I've blamed myself for his death for years."

"Why?"

"Young Billy had just gotten out of high school, and he was doing what we used to call 'sowing wild oats.'" He peers over at me. "You know what that means?"

"Sort of."

"Well, he was doing what most young folk do. Acting all wild and crazy. Drinking beer, smoking cigarettes, driving too fast, and staying out late."

"I thought you said he'd gone to church?"

"Oh yes, he'd been raised in the church. But he got lazy about it during his last year of high school. Billy and I used to fight something fierce. And I'd say all sorts of terrible things to him." Mr. Campton rubs his hand across his chin and sighs.

"I can't imagine you doing that."

"Oh, believe me, I did. I used to tell him that he'd

come to no good. That he was a worthless, useless, hopeless excuse for a man. All that and worse." Mr. Campton sighs sadly. "Well, he and I had a terrible blowup one night when he came home real late. I got mad and told him he ought to go enlist himself in the service—let them make a man out of him. You see, I'd done my time over in the Pacific during the war. Seemed like a good idea for Billy to go and do the same."

"And he did?"

"Yep. He went out and signed himself up in the army the very next day. Him and a buddy. Within the same month he went off to boot camp. He was shipped to 'Nam the end of August. And shot down in a rice paddy just a month later. September 22. Always remember that day."

"I'm sorry."

"Me too. It took me a while to realize that God forgave me. Then I had to work on forgiving myself. Billy had written a letter from boot camp, assuring us that he was shaping up and had been going to church and reading his Bible and praying. That was something."

"Yeah."

"But it's still hard."

"I can imagine." And I can. I just can't imagine ever getting over it. How do you really get over something like this? Both Nana and Mr. Campton have mentioned God as the answer, but even so I cannot imagine that God—if he's even there at all— would care about someone as worthless as me.

I think about going to see Nana this afternoon.

I could still make it during visiting hours. But despite the buzzing in my head I feel exhausted. I just want to sleep. I lean my head back against the wooden chair and close my eyes. I can hear Mr. Campton talking still. He's saying something about God, I think, or maybe Jesus, but I can't quite process his words. Even so, they're like this gentle wave that washes over me. Not unpleasant really, just a kind of nothingness.

When I wake up, I'm alone. I pick up my flower jar and go into the apartment. It's already past six. I think it's safe to visit Sammy's grave now.

I wrap the flower jar in old newspapers and carefully place it in my backpack, arranging and padding it so the blooms won't be crushed. But as I bike across town, I feel the water sloshing out and dripping down my lower back in a cold wet stream.

I can't remember ever feeling this weak and tired as I finally pedal up the hill toward the cemetery. It's not even a steep hill—just an incline. Nothing like the one that Sammy and I used to race up, back when we were both alive and well. My feet feel like lead weights as I lift and push them against the pedals. Finally, I must stop. I climb off my bike and simply wheel it up the final block. If I cared I'd be embarrassed by my lack of stamina.

I wonder if I will be able to find his grave, but

figure it will be the fresh one—the one with all the
flowers. I park my bike without locking it and continue trudging along, one foot in front of the other.
I'm thinking I should have on my old-man outfit
because that's just how I feel. Then I come to an
area that looks well maintained. I see a grave with
lots of flowers and pick up my pace, as if I'm actually meeting him here. Like we're going to have
some sort of clandestine rendezvous.

But when I'm just a few graves away, I see her.
She steps out from behind an oak tree and fully into
my view. Her back is turned to me, but I recognize
her perfectly styled blonde hair and the black suit
she wore to the funeral. Very chic considering the
circumstances, but then Kyra has a way of making
anything look stylish.

I freeze in midstep, terrified that she will turn
and see me. And then I wonder why. Why should
I be afraid of Sammy's sister? Maybe this is meant
to be. Maybe this is the moment when Kyra and
I will finally come back together, our friendship
reunited by the guy we both loved so dearly. Maybe
this is my big chance to explain everything to her—
how sorry I am, what a fool I was, how much I
loved Sammy, how my life will never be the same
without him. I take another step forward, and then
she turns. She looks startled.

But I keep walking slowly, as if I'm approaching
a wary animal. I'm straining my brain for something to say. Something that will make a chink in
this iceberg floating between us. But what kind of
greeting do you use under such circumstances?

Hey? Hi? Hello? None seem fitting. But I soon discover I don't need any words. Kyra is ready to do all the talking.

"What are *you* doing here?" she demands.

I open my mouth to speak, but she cuts me off.

"Can't you see that we don't want you coming around here?" She glares at me now—as if I'm the devil himself. "You have absolutely no right to be at my brother's graveside, *Miranda Sanchez.*" She speaks my name as if it is bitter arsenic. "You're the reason he's dead, you know. *Sammy is dead because of you!*" And then she begins to cry—and this hits me even harder than her words.

I take another step forward, thinking—perhaps in a delusional way—that I can comfort her now that she's sobbing uncontrollably.

"Stay away from me!" she screams, holding out her hands as if to keep me at bay. "And stay away from Sammy. Isn't it bad enough that you helped bring on his death—can't you leave him alone now that he's six feet under?"

I back away from her now, my dripping backpack hanging limply from one hand. I still consider saying something like "I'm sorry." But I have a feeling it doesn't matter to her. That nothing I can say will make any difference or change anything. Of course not. Why am I so incredibly stupid?

I notice my eyes are blurry as I climb onto my bike. But I don't care. It's probably because it's getting dusky out. I start to pedal, thinking, *Mission aborted—get away while you can.* I let gravity pull me down the decline. I wish it could pull me down,

down, down forever. Where would it take me?
To hell, perhaps?

As I coast down the street, something wet streaks
across my cheeks, hot and then cold. I finally realize
it's my own tears. It occurs to me that Kyra's harsh
words were really a gift. She was able to cut me
deeply enough to unleash an emotion I thought I'd
forgotten. I have remembered how to cry.

My chest is heaving up and down by the time
I finally stop at the city park. I dismount my bike
and walk it down a path, sobbing with each step.
My nose is dripping and I just let it. The park is
empty so no one is around to witness my scene.
Not that I care. I finally reach the area where Sammy
and I used to practice soccer together. I drop my
bike to the ground and flop down on my stomach
beside it. It feels as if everything inside me is breaking loose now, pouring itself out like a flood from a
broken dam. I sob into the damp grass and soil, my
tears mixing with the dew. How I wish I could melt
into the ground too—just pour everything out and
simply cease to exist. Is it possible?

When I awake, it's completely dark. I'm not sure if
I've fallen asleep or had some sort of seizure, but I
feel cold and wet and empty. I stand stiffly to my
feet and wipe my face on the hood of my sweatshirt.
I consider leaving my flowers right here in the park
as a way to honor Sammy's memory. But somehow
it doesn't feel quite right. And yet I don't want to go
back to the cemetery either. It's clear I've been ban-
ished from there. I try to think of a place that really

holds meaning for Sammy and me. And then it hits me. I remember the night of the snowman—the night of the snowy kiss.

I put on my soggy backpack, climb back onto my bike, and pedal over to BigMart. I ride straight over to the west side of the parking lot where, fortunately, there aren't too many cars, even though the store is still open and the middle section of the parking lot is fairly full. It's nothing like that deserted night in January. Why didn't I realize how special that night was at the time? Why didn't I just grab Sammy and hold on tight? Why didn't I keep kissing him until morning? Why didn't I tell him that I loved him? Or even ask him to marry me? I'm sure he would've said yes. Of course, he'd have also said, "Let's wait until after graduation, Randi." But I'm sure he'd have agreed. And then none of this would've happened. Now I'm destined to be alone forever. For as long as I live I'll always be wishing he were here with me. Oh, why am I so incredibly stupid?

I take off my backpack and remove the soggy bundle. In the glow of the lamplight above me I peel away wet layers of newspaper to discover that the flowers still look fairly good and there's some water left in the jar. I think, *This is the exact spot where we kissed that night, as best as I can remember, right under the lamppost here.* So I set down my offering. Then I sit down on the pavement, lean against the lamppost, and begin talking to Sammy.

"Sammy, I am so, so, so sorry." I pause and look up to the sky, but all I see is the brightness of the light with blackness all around it. "I know the word *sorry* doesn't even begin to cut it. But I am. And if I could do anything—I mean *anything*—to bring you back here, I would. I mean it, Sammy. I would do anything. I was such a total fool. Can you hear me, Sammy? Do you know how much I love you? Do you know how badly I'm hurting right now? Do you know how sorry I am? Do you know how empty my life has become without you?"

I stop speaking when a mom and two little kids pause to stare at me. She keeps her kids close to her as she fumbles to unlock the door of her minivan. She eyes me as if I might actually be slightly nuts, perhaps wondering if I will harm her or her children. I look away and wait for them to leave.

Then I continue speaking—with an urgency now, as if I only have him on the line for a few more moments. "I have this plan, Sammy." I lower my voice in case anyone out here is listening. "I am going to join you. Soon. I can't do it right now because Nana—remember Nana? Well, she's better right now. She's got some new medication that's helping her remember. So I don't want to mess it up for her. But when she's strong enough, I'll do it, Sammy. I have several ideas of how. And I know that I can. I really know that I can. You have no idea how much it comforts me to know that I can do this thing. And that I'll be with you." I stare down at the crack in the pavement where a weed is starting to grow. "There's just one problem, Sammy. I don't really know where you are right now. So I'm not totally sure that I'll join you if I kill myself. I mean you are *so* good, Sammy. And I am so—so bad. I'm just not completely sure that I'll make it wherever you are. *Where are you, Sammy?*"

An older couple is getting into a big RV that's parked nearby. The woman's cell phone is in her hand. She's staring at me like she thinks I'm crazy, and I wonder if she's going to call the police or something. So I climb back onto my bike and ride for home. As I pedal I decide that it may not even matter whether I actually get to see Sammy again or not. If I'm not good enough to go wherever he is, I'll just have to take whatever I get. Whatever I deserve. And maybe that's a good thing. Or at least fair. Besides, I'm sure whatever I get couldn't hurt any more than this.

Shelby sees me from the kitchen window as I park my bike on the front porch. She smiles and waves like all is right with the world. Trying desperately to imitate her, I wave back. But I know I look pitiful. Then I go into Nana's apartment, find the other blue pill, and, without the aid of water, swallow it. I lie down on Nana's bed without removing my still-damp clothes and fall asleep.

Somehow, the next morning I get up and make it to school in time for Mitch's first-period class. I suppose I have an ulterior motive now. I'm all out of pills. I sit in the back again, avoiding eye contact and conversation with everyone. No one seems to care or even notice that I'm missing . . . and I know I am definitely missing. I stay in my seat until the room is empty, then quickly move forward.

Mitch frowns as I approach his desk. "You're still not looking too good this morning, Miranda."

"Yeah." I glance toward the door. "I need some more of those pills."

"Oh . . . I don't know."

"Look, it's the only thing that's keeping me going right now," I state simply. Then, using my backup plan, I add, "And if you don't give me the pills I might have to talk to Detective Sanders."

His brows lift. "Blackmail?"

"Whatever."

Then he smiles in a mischievous sort of way. "This is a whole new side of you, Miranda. I think maybe I like it."

I narrow my eyes.

"Come by the shop after school." He watches as kids start coming in. "Same time as last."

With this knowledge I manage to make it through the day. And after school I go to the park and wait around until I'm sure that Mitch will be at the bike shop. When I get there, Mitch is finishing up with some customers. Finally they leave, and I approach Mitch. But just as we begin talking, two more people enter the shop—Tyrone Larson and his hillbilly friend Hale Ramsey. I'd run into them from time to time at Mitch's shop, which always struck me as slightly odd. I can't imagine either Tyrone or Hale being into biking.

"Hey, Miranda," says Tyrone, eyeing me up and down like he's never seen me before. I wonder if he likes what he sees or is as disgusted with my lack of hygiene and fashion sense as Kyra would be.

Hale doesn't seem to mind, though. He's grinning like I'm fresh meat straight off the farm. "Howdee there, Miss Mirandy," he drawls.

I nod briskly to both of them, then fix my gaze back on Mitch.

"Not very friendly now, are you?" Hale walks over to me until he's just inches from my face. "According to Mitch, you should be a mite more friendly, Miss Mirandy. Or are you too good for the likes of us?"

I glare at him. "My name is *Miranda.*"

"Well, 'scuse the fur offa me."

"Never mind him," says Tyrone, giving Hale a shove. "Lay off, man."

Mitch clears his throat now. "Look, Miranda, these guys are here for a reason. I can't help you with—well, you know. But these guys can. So I just thought I'd offer a formal introduction of sorts." He kind of laughs now. "Although I'm sure you guys have all met before."

I look from Mitch to Tyrone to Hale, then back to Mitch again. "But you said—"

"Hey, I didn't promise you anything."

"But what about the—?"

"This is the best way for everyone, Miranda." Mitch steps up now and places both hands on my shoulders as he catches my eyes with a warm intensity. "Just trust me on this, okay?"

Disappointed, I nod. I know there's no point in standing against him on this. And really all I want from him now are the pills—just enough to get me by. I guess it doesn't matter who I get them from.

Although I probably never would've had much to do with these two characters in the past. But as I look at Tyrone and Hale again, it suddenly occurs to me that they're not all that different from me. Uninvolved, slightly checked out, generally losers. Maybe we three do belong together after all. Maybe this is meant to be.

"Fine," I say. "Whatever."

"Now that's the right attitude," Hale crows.

The little bell on the door jingles, and Mitch glances nervously toward the front of the store. "Think you can take this someplace else now?"

"Sure 'nough, pardner," Hale says.

And the three of us exit out the back. Hale walks over to an old pea-green car that's seen better days, leans against the hood, and rolls out a cigarette, as neat as you please, right on the knee of his Wranglers. He lights up and blows a puff of smoke right into my face. I take a couple of steps away and glare back at him but say nothing.

"So what're you looking for?" Hale asks.

"Huh?"

"You know, what do you need?"

I frown now. Feeling stupid, I realize that I really don't know much drug language, street terms or otherwise. I don't even know what the name of the stuff that Mitch gave me was. Still I don't want to look too dumb. "Mostly I need something to help me sleep. And something to get me going. You know?"

Tyrone shifts, and all of a sudden I notice that he seems uncomfortable.

"So you're not really into this for fun then?" Hale asks.

"I'm just trying to get by," I say quickly.

"So how much do you need?" Hale asks again as he takes a puff on his cigarette.

"I'm not sure."

"Well, what can you afford?" Hale asks more brusquely.

Now this is the first time it's occurred to me that this stuff is going to cost me. Up until now it's been free. I briefly wonder what in the world I'm doing here, standing in a back parking lot, making a drug deal. It seems out of character and slightly ridiculous. But then life is like that. It can change in a heartbeat. Still, this doesn't feel like my life anymore. It doesn't feel like life at all.

"I guess I just want a week's worth," I finally say. Then it occurs to me that I could get what I need to end everything while I'm at it. "Oh, well, why don't you just make it a month's worth?"

"A month?" Hale tightens up his face like he's doing some kind of mental math and then tosses out a figure. A surprisingly large figure.

I'm sure I look slightly stunned.

"Too much?"

"No, it's okay." I peer around the parking lot. "Naturally, I don't have it on me."

Hale laughs. "Yeah, you and me both."

"What do I—?"

"I can make a delivery. You still in that apartment where you had the party?"

"Yeah. But I live downstairs now. Apartment 1A."

"You going to be home tonight?"

"Yeah." I roll my eyes. "It's not like I'm going anywhere."

"Cool." Hale snuffs out his cigarette beneath the heel of his cowboy boot and calls out, "You about ready to hit the road, Ty?"

"Yeah." Tyrone eyes me again. "You need a ride?"

"No, I'm on my bike."

"Okay," Tyrone says softly. "See ya later."

I decide to stop by to visit Nana before I go home. I feel bad for neglecting her yesterday. But when I look for her in the dayroom and then out-side, I don't see her anywhere. I wonder if it's possi-ble they've released her. I shudder to think what she'll do if she sees what a mess I've made of her little apartment. I hurry over to the nurse I spoke to the other day.

"I'm looking for Helen Bartlett," I quickly explain.

The nurse frowns. "She's not doing too well today."

"What do you mean?"

"She's in bed. That experimental medication seemed to be making her sick. Her blood pressure was dangerously high, and we were getting worried about the possibility of a stroke. Unfortunately that's one of the most common side effects with that particular drug."

"Can I see her?"

She nods. "But be warned, she probably won't know you."

I am flooded with guilt as I walk to Nana's room.

I replay my last conversation with her, how I promised I would visit. And then I let one precious day slip by, and now who knows what?

"Nana?" I speak quietly as I stand by her bed. She doesn't even look like the same woman. She has an IV in one arm and a blood-pressure cuff on the other. Her eyes are barely open, and there is no recognition in them.

"Is it breakfast time?" she mumbles.

I shake my head. "Nana. It's Miranda, your granddaughter. Do you remember me?"

She looks confused now. It's a look I've seen way too many times before. For the second time in two days, my eyes fill up with tears. I hold Nana's hand and quietly cry. I wonder if I will ever get life right. Or should I just call it quits now?

Finally I leave. As I ride away from the nursing home, I know there is nothing left to live for. No one left to disappoint. A month's supply of sleeping pills should do the trick.

18

It occurs to me that Hale probably won't want me to write him a check for the pills. I don't recall ever seeing a drug deal on TV or in the movies where they paid by check. Usually it's a suitcase full of cash, but I won't need that much. Anyway, I decide I better swing by the bank before it closes and withdraw the money from my account. It's not like I'll be needing it for anything else. The teller at the bank counts out my cash without even blinking. For some reason I thought she'd wonder why I was taking out so much. But then it's her job to give the customer what the customer wants. And this customer wants to go buy drugs—and check out.

I stuff the bills into my backpack and leave, but I'm barely out the swinging glass door before I literally run into Dylan Gray.

When I see him, I'm in shock. For some reason
I always equate Dylan with Kyra—probably because
they've always been so close—so I assume Dylan will
treat me the same way Kyra has. I cringe, ready to
make a run for it before I get verbally blasted again.

"Miranda," he says, as if I'm an old friend.

I blink and take another step back, certain that
this is a trick. Maybe Kyra's lurking around the
corner, ready to launch another attack.

"I haven't seen you around much lately," he
continues kindly.

"Yeah." I focus on a crack in the sidewalk and
wish it would open up and swallow me.

"I thought you'd come to the funeral."

I bite my lip and say nothing.

"Look, I can tell you're not doing so well." He
puts his hand on my shoulder now. "This is hard
on everyone, but I'll bet it's really killing you."

I look up at him now. Is he sincere or just setting
me up?

"We're having a get-together. At the church.
It's just Sammy's close friends, kind of our way to
remember him, you know. Something the Sam Man
would really appreciate."

I feel this tiny spark of hope. Like a drowning
person who's getting a life preserver tossed her way.

"You've got to come, Miranda. Sammy would
definitely want you there."

Tears fill my eyes again. I'm starting to wonder if
I'll cry like this every day now for the rest of my life.
"I'd like to come," I manage to croak out.

"Cool. It's at seven, in the youth house."

I wipe my wet cheeks with the back of my hand. "Sounds good."

"Yeah, we're even going to have a birthday cake."

"Oh, that's right." It hits me like a slap in the face that tomorrow Sammy would've been 18. Then I remember something else—something that makes it feel like my fingers have just slipped off the life preserver. "That means it's Kyra's birthday too."

"Yeah," Dylan says. "It's going to be a tough one for her."

"So, of course, Kyra will be there."

"Yeah."

"I better not come, Dylan." I hear the tremor in my voice.

"No, you *need* to be there, Miranda."

I step away from him. "You don't understand. It would spoil everything for Kyra if I showed up. Really. She's made it perfectly clear that—"

"You *need* to come, Miranda. For yourself as well as Kyra. And what about Sammy? This is to honor him, you know."

I take another step back. "No, Dylan. It would be wrong. So wrong." And then I turn and start biking away. Before I know it I'm pedaling as fast as I can. I want to get away from Dylan Gray. I can't stand his pity. It's starting to melt me.

By the time I get home I'm exhausted. I flop down on the couch, wishing for sleep, but my head throbs and my heart races. I can barely breathe. I don't know how long I lie there, but when I get up it's dark inside and out. I turn on some lights and decide to forage for something to eat. It occurs to me that I haven't eaten anything all day. No wonder I can barely operate. I finally settle on an old micro-wave dinner, but when I open the microwave I'm greeted by a stench that makes me want to vomit. Apparently Nana mistakenly put a carton of ice cream in the microwave before she went into the nursing home. Naturally this makes sense because I'd already removed the cup of coffee from the freezer. She was always doing things like this. Putting laundry soap in the dryer or her gloves on her feet. I usually came in after school to make sure nothing too frightening had been confused or mis-placed. Somehow I'd overlooked the microwave.

I finally manage to clean up the reeking mess, but now I have no appetite for a microwave meal. I hunt around until I find a box of crackers and a can of sardines. This used to be one of Nana's favor-ite snacks. How intimidated I was the first time I saw those tiny fishes with heads and fins still intact! But it wasn't long before Nana had me gobbling them down too. I manage to consume more than half the can and as many crackers as before I hear a knock on the door.

I peer out the window to see that it's Hale and Tyrone.

My heart begins to pound as I invite them in. I realize that I am actually participating in a real drug deal right now, and that I could land in jail if I were to get busted. But then I realize that it's quite likely I'll land in jail anyway, when I get convicted of whatever degree of murder the D.A. finally settles on. So what does it matter, really?

"Interesting place you got here," Tyrone says as he looks around.

I follow his gaze as he takes in Nana's funny old crocheted throws, various pieces of floral porcelain, and old-fashioned prints on the wall.

"It was my grandma's place," I explain. "I'm just staying here for a while."

"By yourself?" asks Hale.

I nod.

"Well, doesn't that just make you wanna slap your mama?"

"Huh?"

Tyrone rolls his eyes. "Just another one of Hale's—"

"Watch yourself!" snaps Hale. His eyes instantly fill with anger.

It disturbs me, but I pretend not to notice. I suspect Tyrone was about to mention something regarding Hale's hillbilly heritage. Although, personally, I'm not totally convinced that Hale really is such a hick. Sometimes I think it's just a big act to get attention. And who would know, since he moved here from another state. Maybe he just relocates from state to state, constantly reinventing himself along the way. Come to think of it, that's not such a bad idea.

"So does your mom still live upstairs?" asks Tyrone.

Now I wonder how he knows so much about me and my mom since he's only been to my place once that I can recall, the night of the party.

"Yeah. Shelby still lives upstairs. But she checks

on me pretty regularly." I know it's a lie, but for some reason I'd like them to believe I'm not as isolated as I am. "And the neighbor next door, Mr. Campton, thinks it's his personal responsibility to keep an eye on me too. So it's not like I'm completely on my own, you know."

"Yeah, but being on your own is pretty cool." Tyrone removes a pile of my stuff that's still heaped everywhere and drops it on the floor. Then he sits down in Nana's old dusty-rose recliner. But he seems antsy, as if he's not quite comfortable with being here.

"Make yourself at home," I say as I lean against an armchair.

Hale has already flopped down onto the camel-hair sofa, his long legs sprawling in front of him in a way that reminds me of a giant grasshopper.

"Hey, we got us a six-pack in the truck," Hale suggests. "We could make this into a *real* party."

I briefly consider this. It occurs to me that I haven't had a single sip of alcohol since the night Sammy died. I'm not even sure why, since I obviously have no qualms about buying illegal drugs. But the mere memory of the taste of it—maybe all those times of barfing it up—just leaves me cold now. "No thanks."

"Aw, come on, Mirandy—"

"Hale, I *told* you the name's Miranda," I snap.

He holds up his hands like I've got a gun on him. "Sorry, *Miranda*. You know, you could really use a beer to help you lighten up."

I think about this. He's probably right. I do feel

pretty uptight. Besides, it might help to get this deal over with sooner. It might be one of those things where you've got to raise your glass with the thugs. And what could it really hurt anyway? I'm sure that Shelby's out tonight, since it's a Friday, her night to hang loose. Not that she'd care anyway. Finally I say, "Yeah, sure, whatever."

"Cool." Hale nods toward Tyrone, and Tyrone jumps to his feet.

"Don't let anyone see you bringing it in here," I warn. Then I wonder why, since I sure didn't seem to care a week ago. Was it really only a week ago? How can that even be possible?

Hale laughs now. "Don't you worry none, little filly. Me and Ty know how to play our cards close to our chest."

Something about the way Hale talks literally makes my skin crawl. And it's funny because it's not that I don't like a good Southern drawl or even country music when no one's around to catch me listening. I even bought a Dixie Chicks CD once. But the stuff that comes out of Hale's mouth feels as slimy as his overly gelled hair looks greased. I just can't get past it.

Tyrone comes back carrying a grocery bag. *"Voila!"* he announces as he pulls out a six-pack. "How's that for discreet?"

"Thanks." It's funny how being seen with some-one like Hale can suddenly make someone like Tyrone seem lots more appealing. I wonder if this isn't Tyrone's tactic. Why else would anyone hang with Hale? But then why should I care? Once I get

what I need from these two goons, they are out of
here. And I won't ever have to be nice to them
again.

Midway through my second beer, Hale begins
to talk business. I suspect he's worried that I might
get too loopy and forget about our little drug deal.
And I must admit that this beer is hitting me a little
harder than usual. Maybe it's this particular brand
or because I haven't had any alcohol for a while.
Or maybe it's just the combination of beer with the
pills in my system. I've heard you're not supposed
to mix your prescriptions with alcohol. Like these
pills are a prescription! Get real.

Finally I retrieve the cash from my backpack
and count it out into Hale's hand. Just like the
bank teller did today. And like a good druggist he
produces a little white bag. "The orange ones are
to take during the day, and the white ones are for
night."

"Orange if by day and white if by night." I hold
up two fingers and laugh at my sloshy Paul Revere
imitation, but no one else seems to get it. Then I
hold up my bottle of beer and down the remains in
one long swig. "Well, thank you very much, boys."
I stand up now.

"You mean that's it?" Hale looks slightly aggra-
vated. "Partee's over? Just like that?"

"Yep," I say. "You got your money. I got my
pills. Time to call it a night."

"Aw, come on." Hale tries to use his enticing
voice again. "It's not even late."

But I'm not interested. I walk over to the door

and open it wide. "Here's your hat, boys, what's your hurry?"

Hale cusses. "You ain't much fun, Mirandy."

As Tyrone rises to his feet, I glare at Hale for using that name. "Never said I was."

"It's not always what you say, you know." Hale slams his empty beer bottle so hard on Nana's glass-topped coffee table that I hear it crack. Now I'm really mad. I point out the door.

"What're you going to do next time you need something to help you through, Miranda?" Hale asks as he walks past me.

"Maybe there won't be a next time," I say quickly.

Hale laughs at this. "Yeah, that's what everybody thinks."

Tyrone is strangely quiet. And looks at me almost sadly.

Finally they leave, and I slam the door behind them. Then I lock it. My hands are shaking as I go straight to the bag and look inside. There is one plastic bag with orange pills and another with white. White if by night.

I pop a white pill into my mouth and go to the sink for a drink of water. By the time I come back into the living room I can already feel my head starting to swim, but I'm sure it must be the beer. . . .

The following morning, I wake up still on the couch. Nana's apartment looks worse than ever. The empty beer bottles and cracked coffee table don't help much either. I think about how Nana would feel if she unexpectedly came home to find it like this, and I start crying. This is wrong. Wrong in so many ways.

I take an orange pill and jump into the shower. And when I come out it's like I'm doing everything in fast motion as I whip around the apartment trying to clean the place up. Before long I realize that this cleanup is really twofold. One is out of respect for Nana. But also, if I really take all those white pills tonight, I need to leave this place neat and orderly for Shelby's sake. After all, I want to do this thing right. I want everything in perfect order. Anything else would be selfish.

I notice Mr. Campton standing out in a corner of the backyard as I take the trash out. I try to slip away without being seen but it's too late.

"Miranda!" His voice sounds urgent. "Come here at once!"

Worried that he might be having a heart attack or seizure or something, I race to his side. "What's wrong?"

"Look!" He's bent over, pulling back the lower branches of the juniper shrub.

I kneel down to see better. There, in what appears to be a nest of sorts, are three tiny kittens of varying colors. But as I look closer, two appear not to be moving at all. In fact, they seem to be completely lifeless. But the third one, a soft gray color, moves slightly. I stare without speaking.

"Are they okay?" he asks.

"I don't know." Finally I force myself to reach into their protected little nest. I touch the calico with a finger, but it feels cold and stiff. I touch the tiny

tiger-stripe to find it feels exactly the same. I jerk
my hand back and stand up, looking at Mr. Campton
for some sort of explanation.

"Are they dead?" he asks with worried eyes.

I nod without speaking, and tears gather again.

He shakes his head sadly. "All of them?"

"One might be alive, at least I think it is." Then
I look back down to make sure I didn't just imagine
it. Maybe I'm wrong. Maybe all three are dead. But
I notice that the gray's head is moving just slightly
to the left and right, as if the poor thing is looking
for something. Probably his mother.

"What happened here?" I demand. I place my
hands on my hips and stare at Mr. Campton as if
he's personally responsible for this feline tragedy.
Or at least for subjecting me to more pain. Like I
need more pain!

"Well, I saw the old feral cat, the mother, out on
the street this morning. She's dead. Must've been run
over last night. I was worried about the kittens. They
don't last long without a mother. No warmth. No
food."

I bend over now and scoop up the little gray.
He is as light as a dust bunny. "What do I do now?"
I demand.

"My wife, God bless her soul, rescued a kitten
with an eyedropper once. You warm up the milk and
feed it from an eyedropper."

"I don't have any milk. Or an eyedropper."

"I do."

I follow Mr. Campton into his apartment. It's the
first time I've ever been inside, but I don't even

bother to look around. My eyes are on this tiny kitten. Before long Mr. Campton has rounded up an eyedropper and is warming up some milk in his microwave.

"You've got to test it on your wrist like this," he tells me as he dips his finger into the cup of milk, then touches it to his wrist. "Used to have to do this when our kids were babies. So it's not too hot." He hands me the eyedropper now. "You better feed this little one, Miranda. My eyes are so bad that I'd probably miss his mouth or maybe put out an eye."

And so I fill the eyedropper. Then, holding the kitten in one hand, I offer him the milk from the glass tube, trying to drip it into his mouth although most seems to be going down his chin. But it doesn't take too long before he figures it out. He seems to be a survivor. Slowly he laps down what appears to be maybe a couple of teaspoonfuls. "Do you think that's enough?" I ask.

"Yeah, I think so. For now anyway. You don't want him to overdo it. But you'll have to keep feeding him off and on all day long. And keep him warm."

"How often should I feed him?"

Mr. Campton rubs his chin. "Maybe every one or two hours to start with. Not too much though. His little tummy might explode."

"Really?"

"Well, it might make him sick. This is cow's milk, you know. Might take him a while to get used to it."

"And that's all I do. Just feed him and keep him warm?"

"I reckon. But don't get your hopes too high, Miranda. He still might not make it."

"Should I call a vet?"

"Don't know that it'd help much to start with. If the little guy holds on through the weekend, you might take him in on Monday."

"What about when I'm at school?"

"Hmm. If my eyes were better I'd help you—"

"Or maybe I can sneak him in." I pull out my sweatshirt pocket and gently tuck the kitten inside. "Do you think anyone will notice?"

Mr. Campton grins. "Nah, I don't see how. Why, it's just like a kangaroo pouch."

And so I spend the rest of my day cleaning Nana's apartment and caring for my new little charge. I know it's probably wrong, and fortunately I won't need to tell anyone about this, but for the time being I'm calling him Samuel.

I putter around Nana's apartment, doing a
better job of cleaning than I have ever done in my
life. I feel like the Energizer Bunny, but at the same
time sort of uneven and jerky, like if I'm not careful
I might just topple over. It's not such a good feeling
really. If I planned to live a long and full life, I'd
have to quit these pills altogether. But they seem
to keep me going for the time being, and I guess
I have no reason to worry about side effects. What
should it matter?

Samuel is resting comfortably in my sweatshirt
pocket. At regular intervals I stop to warm the milk
that Mr. Campton gave me. Then I carefully drop
it into the kitten's tiny mouth. My aim is getting
better, and he is learning to actually suck on the
dropper now. I talk to him too. I try to make myself

sound like his mother, but I'm not sure who I'm really fooling here.

By late afternoon I realize that Samuel has definitely put a kink in my plans. If I take those pills tonight, as planned, who will take care of Samuel tomorrow? Certainly not Shelby. She'd send him to the pound for sure. So I hide my little white bag of pills in a drawer that sticks in Nana's old bureau, and I promise myself that the time will come eventually. My escape is only a bag away. As soon as Samuel is strong enough to be given away, I will find him a good home. And I will depart from this one. It feels a little strange to be thinking these thoughts in such a matter-of-fact way. And yet it brings me comfort too. It's like I have some control.

At 6:30 I hear someone knocking on my door. At first I feel worried that it's Hale and Tyrone, looking for a place to party again. Now I wish I'd never let them into Nana's apartment. But when I peer through the peephole, I'm surprised to find that it's Jamie.

I open the door and stare at him. "What are you doing here?"

"I went upstairs to look for you first, but your mom said you'd moved down here." He glances over my shoulder with interest. "Cool. You have your own place now. Didn't your grandma used to live here before?"

"Yeah." I open the door wider. "Wanna come in?"

"Sure."

"So, what's up?" I ask him as we both stand awkwardly just inside the door. I don't know why I don't invite him to sit down. But I suppose I'm guessing that he's just passing by. I can't imagine he actually stopped by to really visit. I notice he seems to be dressed nicer than usual. Khakis and a navy sweater. It looks good on him.

"I just wanted to talk to you for a minute, Miranda." He glances at his watch now as if he literally means a minute. "I thought I'd stop by and try to talk you into coming to the party—"

"*Party?*" My brows arch at the sound of that word. Partying is so unlike Jamie. "What do you mean—?"

"It's at the church. For Sammy."

"Oh yeah. I heard about that."

"So, why don't you come with me?"

"No way," I say firmly.

"Why?"

I try to think of a light answer. "Well, for one thing I don't feel like getting all dressed up like my grandpa tonight. Been there, done that."

He laughs. "Fine. Why not come as yourself?"

"I can't."

"Why not?"

"Look, Jamie, it's no secret that Kyra doesn't want me around right now. And who could blame her? If it weren't for me Sammy would still be—"

"You're wrong, Miranda. And it's totally crazy for you to keep on hogging all of the blame. Can't you see that we all feel guilty? It just goes with the territory."

"Yeah, I'm sure." I roll my eyes and put my hand on the doorknob, my subtle hint that his mission is useless.

"I'm serious. I've been struggling with a lot of guilt too. Did you know that Sammy asked me to go to your party that night? He wanted me to go with him. He begged me to go, but I refused—"

"Yeah, well, you were smart." I turn the doorknob.

"No!" Jamie grabs me by the arm. "Can't you see it? If I'd gone, I would've been there for him. None of this ever would've happened. Do you know how many times I've played this scene through my head, Miranda?"

"So why didn't you come?"

He looks away. "I don't know."

"But it's not your fault, Jamie."

"Easy for you to say. But you don't know how I feel inside."

"Oh yeah?" I fiddle with the dead bolt. "I think I do—and then some."

"Did you know that Dylan feels guilty too? He'd made plans to do something with Sammy after the play that night, but then he bailed on him. And then there's Kyra. Believe it or not, she blames herself too."

"Kyra?" I shake my head. "No way. If anyone is totally blameless here, it's Kyra. Next to Sammy, she's the biggest victim of this whole nightmare. And that's why I can't go tonight."

"You don't know everything about this, Miranda."

"Does anyone?"

"Maybe Sammy."

I consider this. Does he really know everything now? Or is he just asleep? Or what exactly?

"Besides—" Jamie continues in what I'm sure he thinks is a convincing tone—"what about the creep who gave him the dope? Or the idiot who manufactures that junk in the first place? I'll bet you didn't invite those morons to your party, did you?"

"Not that I know of. But I obviously let them in the door."

"Hey, there were a lot of other people there that night, Miranda. You can't take the blame for everything that happened," he says. "Even Mitch was there," he adds, his eyes narrowing.

I know Jamie's never been very fond of Mitchell Wade. He seemed suspicious of Mitch from the very beginning. But I never knew why. I assumed Jamie was just jealous of Mitch's ability to dazzle the girls.

"Come on, Miranda. Come with me tonight. Do it for Sammy. It's what he would want. You gotta know that."

I feel myself being swayed now. And I know Jamie is mostly right. Sammy probably *would* want me there. At least I think so. And it's not that I don't want to go. I just don't want to be seen. Particularly by Kyra. "Oh, I don't know . . ."

"Come on. It'll be good for you."

I sigh, feeling myself, despite myself, giving in to him. I am such a wimp. "Okay, I guess I could go."

"All right!"

"But if Kyra so much as lifts an eyebrow, I'm leaving. Okay? And I don't want you to leave with me. I can walk. It's not that far home."

He seems to think this over, then finally agrees.

"Okay." Then he looks at me. "You ready to go now?"

"You mean do I want to change my clothes first? Clean up a little?"

He shrugs. "Hey, you look fine to me."

"Yeah, and I know Sammy wouldn't mind either. But it might go better with Kyra if I put a little more effort into it."

He smiles now. "Yeah, you know Kyra—Macon High Fashion Police. She might cite you with disorderly dressing."

I try to smile but can't quite make my mouth do that trick. Then I remember something. "Hey, you want to hold this for me while I change?"

"Huh?"

I gently pull little Samuel from my pocket. "It's just a kitten."

"Oh, man." Jamie holds his hands in a cup as I place Samuel there. "He is so tiny. Where'd you get him?"

"His mama got run over. The other kittens were dead. He's the only survivor."

"Cool. You going to keep him?"

"Yeah. For now."

Then I go into Nana's bedroom and try to figure out what to put on. But all I can do is stare at the bed. I long to climb in. I don't think I have what it takes to do this tonight. I don't know why I agreed. I glimpse myself in the big mirror over Nana's bureau and cringe. No way! I cannot do this.

Then I spy the drawer, the one that sticks. I open it with a loud squeak and remove the white bag.

Until now I've limited myself to one pill to get me going, one pill to help me sleep—and that's it. But I think tonight may call for an extra push. I pop an orange pill in my mouth and swallow it. Then, feeling like maybe I can pull this off, I find my best pair of jeans and a clean white T-shirt and change. I pull my hair back with a couple of bungees, then put on a little blush and lip-gloss. I stare at my image again. I look almost human. Almost. I know I need to wear a sweatshirt, for Samuel's sake, but for Kyra's sake I choose a clean one, and in a color that she used to think looked good on me. In fact, I think she picked it out last fall. It's dark burgundy with navy trim. More importantly it has a nice warm front pocket for Samuel.

I can't believe I'm doing this as I climb into the front seat of Jamie's car. It seems even weirder than dressing like my grandpa to go to the funeral. But I can feel my chemical buzz coming, and along with it a sense of confidence. I know it's false, but it's all I have right now.

"Just remember what I said about leaving," I remind Jamie as he parks the car. I recognize several of the other cars already here, and my stomach starts to churn. I put my hands in my front sweatshirt pocket as we walk toward the church. Somehow feeling Samuel nestled there, all soft and warm like that, is a real comfort. Maybe between that and the pill, I can do this thing after all.

I don't see Kyra when I first walk into the youth room, but it's filled with kids I know, or rather used to know. I don't feel that I know them anymore. And

I'm sure they don't know me. I shudder to think what they would think if they did. Not only am I a murderer, but I'm rapidly turning into a drug addict as well. Oh man.

I hear Dylan talking on the other side of the room, reminiscing about Sammy and Kyra's birthday party last year—their 17th. It was a surprise party that Dylan and I had set up at the local Putt-n-Par. We wanted it to feel like a kiddie party, with party hats and balloons and stuff. The theme was hokey. But we had so much fun that night. We all acted goofy and silly, just like five-year-olds. I remember Dylan's little sister, Bethany, came and fit in perfectly. Was that really only a year ago? Anyway, Dylan is retelling the story of how Sammy got a hole in one but managed to put out the clown's eye with the same shot. Fortunately the clown was made of hard molded plastic and the manager of Putt-n-Par didn't make him pay for it when he realized it was an accident as well as Sammy's birthday. Everyone laughs at this, and suddenly I think maybe it was a good idea to come here tonight.

And then I see Kyra. I know she hasn't seen me yet—at least I don't think so—because it almost looks like she's smiling. But not quite, and I can understand that. Still, I try to disappear behind Jamie's left shoulder, which is fairly ridiculous since he's only an inch taller than I am.

"Want some punch?" he offers.

"No," I whisper. "Please, don't move."

He turns and looks at me. "Just relax. It's going to be fine."

I take a deep breath and try to believe him, but in the same instant I know it's hopeless. Kyra has spotted me now. I see her face crease into shadows as she turns to whisper something to Dylan. But he shakes his head as if he's saying no. Then her expression turns really angry—like I'm-going-to-throw-something angry. I've seen Shelby get that exact same look. And I know it's time for me to run.

"Sorry, Jamie," I say quickly. "Gotta go."

"Wait—"

"Nope. I warned you."

And then I'm out of there. I can hear Jamie calling my name, but I am too fast for him. I exit into the hallway and zip around the first right turn and then sprint down the carpeted hall with my hand cradling the kitten as I go. Then when the hallway comes to a T, I take a left and then another right. I have no idea where I am, but I figure at least I'll get away without being followed. A lump crushes my throat, and tears are already pouring down my cheeks, but I don't even care. I can cry all the way home if I want to. I just want to get out of this place—fast. I remember Jamie led us up some stairs to get to the youth room, so I figure I'll take the next staircase going down, then search for one of those green exit signs that are all lit up and split.

"Can I help you?"

I jump at the sound of the woman's voice. Yet it seems slightly familiar. "Huh?" I ask breathlessly.

"Are you lost?"

I study the woman for an instant in the dimly lit hallway and suddenly realize it's Andi Pierce—that barely graduated grief counselor from the high school. "Yeah, you could say that."

"Miranda Sanchez?" She steps closer to see me better.

I nod with what I'm sure must look like a sheepish expression.

"If you're looking for the party, you're going the wrong—"

"No. I'm *leaving* the party. I'm looking for an exit." I wipe my face with my hand. For some reason it bothers me that the grief counselor has caught me crying.

"But didn't it just start?"

"Yeah, for some people. It's over for me."

She frowns. "You wanna talk?"

I want to tell her, "No. I don't wanna talk. I wanna die." And then I get an idea. "Sure," I lie.

"I have an office down this hallway," she offers with a smile.

"You always work on Saturday nights?"

She laughs. "No, I was just picking up a book that I'd left in here. It's on postpartum depression. I'd promised it to a friend who just had a baby and is feeling down." She unlocked the door and flipped on the light. "It's not much, but Pastor Jim lets me use this office for counseling sessions three mornings a week."

"Cool." I try to act enthused, but the office is really just a little windowless box.

"Have a seat."

I sit in an upholstered chair that looks like a garage-sale reject, and she sits in the rocking chair across from me. "I'm going to be honest with you, Andi. I will listen to what you have to say, if you'll let me ask you a favor when we're done."

"Sounds fair to me." She leans back in her chair now. "So what's going on with you tonight, Miranda?"

"Not much." I try to say it casually. "I got talked into coming to this party, but then once I got here I realized it was a bad idea."

"Why's that?"

"Mostly because of Kyra."

"You think she doesn't want you here?"

I restrain myself from saying "duh."

"I know she's having a really hard time, Miranda."

"Yeah. I understand that. I didn't want to spoil this thing for her tonight. I mean, it's her birthday too."

Andi nods. "You're a thoughtful girl."

"No, I'm definitely not a thoughtful girl," I say firmly. "Haven't you heard the news? I am the primary reason that Sammy's not here tonight." I stare at her. "I thought you knew that."

"You're giving yourself a lot of credit, you know."

"You mean for Sammy's death?"

"Yeah. It's like you think you're God or something. Like you alone were the determining factor as to whether or not Sammy James lived or died that night."

"I didn't call 911 when Kyra told me to."

"But Kyra called them herself just minutes later.

Do you think those minutes made that much difference?"

"They do to me. And to Kyra."

"But it probably didn't change anything for Sammy. From what I've heard he was already in a coma."

"But it was my party—" Then the tears come again and I'm unable to speak.

"Yes, I know that. And, believe me, Miranda, I'm not saying you're innocent. I agree with you. You are guilty."

"Really?"

"Yes. We're all a little guilty. And we all need to admit to our mistakes. But some of us are more willing to confess our guilt than others."

For some unexplainable reason I wonder if she's talking about Kyra. But then I don't know how that could be possible.

"And then there are some of us who want to take on the guilt of *everyone* and heap it on ourselves like we're wearing a cement overcoat."

That feels about right.

"I'm not saying that you should pretend to be innocent and go about your happy little life again. I'm just saying you need some forgiveness."

"Forgiveness?" Is this woman from another planet?

She leans forward now. "Look, I don't know where you stand on God, Miranda. But I can tell that you don't have a clue about forgiveness."

"I've asked Sammy to forgive me."

"That's a good start."

"What then?" I put my hand back in my pocket to reassure myself that Samuel is still okay. After all, he's my ulterior motive for talking with Andi tonight. I'm hoping I can convince her to take him for me. Despite this whole counseling thing, I can tell she has a kind heart. I feel sure she'd take good care of him for me.

"You need to ask God to forgive you. And you need to forgive yourself."

I wish I were able to laugh, because that is what I'd like to do right now. I'd like to laugh right in her face. "God? I'm not even sure what I think about God anymore. Or if I even believe in him at all. I used to though. Back when I was little and I went to church with Nana. But Nana's locked up with Alzheimer's now, and Sammy is dead, and frankly, I'm not so sure about God anymore. If he does exist, what kind of person is he?"

"That's a fair question."

"Really?"

She smiles. "Actually, I think any question is a fair question when it comes to God. Too many people don't bother to question him. They just ignore him or believe what someone tells them about him. To really know God you have to come pounding on his door. You have to feel free to ask him your honest questions."

"And will he answer?"

"In his own way and his own time. And you might as well know right up front that his answers might not be the ones you want to hear. But, after all, he's God. He has his reasons." Andi held up her hands. "I don't always understand why he does what he does. Like when my mom died of cancer when I was only 12. What was up with that?"

"But you still believe in him?"

"It's a faith thing," she concludes strongly.

It occurs to me that Andi is the third person this week to bring my troubles to this place—this God place. First it was Nana, then Mr. Campton, and now her. I wonder if it's just a coincidence—or does it mean something? "I just don't get it."

"Yeah. That's why it's a faith thing."

"What do you mean?"

"You've got to believe in him first. Nothing works if you don't believe in him."

"Okay, let's say I believe in him. Then what?"

"Then comes the forgiveness part."

"This feels like a vicious circle to me," I say sarcastically.

She smiles. "Okay, let me take it slow. You believe in God. Then you believe that he made an appearance on earth in the form of his Son, Jesus Christ. He did this so that he could show us how to live and love. Then, finally, he died on the cross to forgive our sins."

"I've never really gotten that part. That dying on the cross to forgive sins. What's the deal with that?" I ask. And for some strange reason, I really do want to know the answer.

"I guess it's kind of like cause and effect. Kind of like if you want something you have to pay for it. Let's see." I can see Andi's really thinking now. "What do you think you deserve for what happened to Sammy?"

I bite into my lip without speaking.

"Come on, Miranda, what do you deserve?"

I stare down at my lap. "To die."

"Okay. So you're thinking it's kind of like a debt then. Like you owe it to Sammy or God or Kyra or whomever to die now. Is that what you're saying?"

I feel my eyes growing wider. I can't believe she gets it. "Yes! That's exactly how I feel."

"Right. And maybe that would be fair—if Jesus weren't in the picture. But what if he died on the cross so God could forgive you? Like God's the judge and Jesus is the D.A., and the D.A. says, 'Okay, we know Miranda is guilty here, but I will take her place.' And the judge says, 'Okay.' Does that make sense?"

"Sort of. But it doesn't seem fair. That I should get off and Jesus should die."

"But that's the part about God being God. He does what he wants and there's not much we can do about it. Other than trust him, that is."

"Well, I appreciate you telling me this. And I guess it makes a little sense." I shift to the edge of my chair, ready to leave now. I'm sure Andi thinks her answers are big enough for me, but I'm still not convinced.

"Now what about that favor, Miranda?"

"Yeah." I pull Samuel from my pocket and hold him out for her to see.

"Oh, how sweet!" She's leaning forward now to see him better. "What a darling. He's so tiny. Is he old enough to be away from his mother?"

I explain about finding him and Mr. Campton and the eyedropper as she pets him with one finger.

"He's so soft." Then she looks at me. "But what's the favor?"

"Well, I-I was wondering if you'd like to have him—to keep."

"But why don't you want to keep him? He's so sweet—he can't be much trouble."

"Well, I need to take care of some things, and I can't take care of him too. But I won't feel good about everything unless he gets a good home." I try to smile at her, but I'm sure it's hopeless. "You seem nice, like you'd love him."

She studies me now, like she's trying to read my mind or my motives or whatever, and suddenly I feel nervous. "Are these things you need to take care of right away, Miranda?"

I nod.

"Like tonight?"

I focus again on my lap and consider just bolting for the door. I know this isn't going to work.

She places both her hands on mine, gently covering Samuel with them. "Miranda, I know what you're planning to do."

"What do you mean?"

"You're thinking about taking your own life, aren't you?"

I look at her now. I feel fresh tears coming, but it doesn't bother me anymore. "What if I am? You said yourself it's what I deserve."

"No," she says intensely. "That's what you *think* you deserve. God's the only one who can determine what we really deserve. And he's already decided to forgive us. That's why Jesus died. So we could be forgiven—clean slate, fresh start."

"It sounds good—a fresh start—but it's just so hard to believe."

"That's why it's called faith." She reaches for a tissue and hands it to me.

"What do you mean?"

"Did you ever hear the story of the mustard seed? The tiny seed that grows into something big? Faith is like that. You come to God with this miniscule particle of faith—something that he gives you in the first place—and then he grows it into something you can build your whole life upon."

I stroke Samuel's fur. "So you don't want my kitten, then?"

"No."

I start to stand.

"Can I ask you something, Miranda?"

I shrug.

"Do you have a real plan?"

"Huh?"

"For how you're going to do it—if you do it, that is?"

"Yeah," I say softly.

"As a counselor, I'm curious. What do you plan to do?"

"Are you going to tell anyone? Do I have client privilege here?" I ask warily.

"I'm a certified counselor. Every client's case is private."

"I have pills."

She nods. "Will you promise me something, Miranda?"

"I don't know. What is it?"

"Would you promise not to do anything until you've really looked into this thing with God?"

"I don't know."

"Okay, how about if we make a deal, then."

"What?"

"You look into this thing with God, and if you still want to take your own life, you come to me and I will keep the kitten for you. Okay?"

"Is this a trick?"

"I give you my word."

"Okay. It's a deal." I glance at the door. "Can I go now?"

"Need a ride?"

"Sure."

And so I get into her Subaru and she drives me home.

"Is that where you live?" she asks as she parks in front of the house.

"Uh-huh."

"I just love this old house. I noticed that it's been made into apartments, but I'm guessing there's nothing available."

"Actually there's one that's vacant—on the second floor."

"But there's no sign out."

"Well, Shelby—that's my mom—she was thinking about selling. But not until summer."

"Do you think she'd rent it out until then? I'm

staying with my parents right now, and it's really starting to wear on everyone."

"I can ask."

"Thanks, Miranda."

I open the car door. "Thank you."

"Remember our deal."

"Okay."

So it doesn't look like I'm going to do it tonight. And I do want to think about some of the stuff that Andi told me. Not that it's going to make any difference. Unless it's true. But that seems pretty hard to believe. I wish I could ask Sammy. I have a feeling he knows by now.

20

Several days have passed since my little "counseling session" with Andi Pierce. It's not that I think she was lying to me, exactly. I guess I'm just not sure. In some ways I feel more confused than ever. But at the same time I have this tiny particle of hope. Maybe *hope*'s not the right word. Maybe it's curiosity. I'm not sure of much of anything anymore. Except that I am currently taking two orange pills per day to get and to keep me going, and two white pills to get to sleep at night. Neither of these really work all that well anymore, yet my life revolves around them. I pretend the orange ones are the sun and the white ones are the moon. And I think about them constantly. It's my primary obsession.

I'm not sure which worries me the most right now—

1. that they're not working so well,

2. that my supply is steadily dwindling, or

3. that I may actually have turned myself into an honest-to-goodness drug addict. Can that happen in two weeks?

The only thing that feels real in my life is Samuel. He gets a little bigger and stronger each day, but he still goes everywhere in my pocket with me. I took him to the vet yesterday, and she said he was probably only four, maybe five weeks old.

"Much too young to be away from his mother," she said with a frown. It felt like she was scolding me, as if I were personally responsible for his orphaning. But then she gave me some vitamins and kitty food and warned me that he was very vulnerable right now. It didn't help when she said, "Good luck." Like I was going to need it. I know she thinks it's somewhat hopeless, like he'll probably die. I could see it in her eyes. But at least she didn't charge me for the visit. That was something. I'm not sure what I'd do if Samuel died. My deal with Andi would be off, that's for sure.

Apparently, Detective Sanders called and left a message on Shelby's phone at work today. Naturally, Shelby wasn't a bit pleased either. "I thought this was all over and done with now," she tells me as she stands out on the porch, shifting from one foot to the other. Then she hands me a plastic bag of groceries. I guess she's concerned that I'm not eating right. "I want you to call her first thing in the morning and straighten this all out. Understand? Do you have any idea how it looks for me to have the police calling me up at work?"

"Not so good?"

"That's right."

"Sorry." I know the quickest way out of a conflict with Shelby is to apologize. Despite her faults, she is usually quick to forgive and forget and move on.

"Well, at least it reminded me that we need to get that phone hooked up in here. Then you can take your own calls. Besides, it'll make me feel better. I'll call the phone company today."

"Thanks." Still I don't know who I would possibly want to call. Well, other than the detective, not that I particularly want to call her.

Now Shelby smiles. "And here's the good news. That Andi Pierce you told me about called. Even though I told her I could only guarantee it until June, she still wants to rent the apartment. It'll be nice to have that extra income."

"Nice," I echo without expression and start to close my door.

"You all right?"

"Sure. Why?"

"I don't know. You just seem different. I mean, you've obviously lost weight—not that it looks bad on you." She squints like she's examining me through a camera lens. "Actually, you might even be able to get a job modeling if you cleaned yourself up a little."

I roll my eyes at her.

"But even besides that, you still just seem different."

"Yeah. Well, I probably am."

"Everything okay at school?"

I nod.

"And with your friends?"

I want to say, "What friends?" but that would only encourage her unwanted concern. It's best to simply play along. "Yeah. I guess we're all still getting over Sammy."

"Well, these things take time."

I wonder how she would even know.

"Let me know if you need anything. Oh yeah," she adds. "Dan's coming over for dinner tonight."

"That'll be nice."

"Did you want to join us?" she asks. "I mean, you can if you want. It's just going to be spaghetti and steaks. I'm not trying to exclude you, Miranda. I just know how you are—"

"No, that's okay. You're right. I wouldn't enjoy it."

"But I'd like you to get to know him better, Miranda." She winks now. "I have a feeling he could be *the one.*"

I try, really hard, to smile. "Good for you."

"Yeah. It's about time, I'd say." Then she happily trips up the stairs with her groceries.

I close the door and sigh. Dan the man. Yeah, it figures.

The next morning, I call Detective Sanders before school, but she's not there yet. I call her again during my lunch break. She answers this time, and I tell her it's me. "My mom said to call you."

"Thank you, Miranda. We've questioned everyone on your list, and I wondered if you could come by and answer a few more questions about a couple of the suspects."

"I've told you everything I know."

"We're not so sure you have."

"What do you mean?"

"Look, Miranda, I don't want to play hardball with you. But you can either come in here willingly, or I can send someone out there to pick you up. Which will it be?"

"I'll come."

"After school?"

"Yeah."

"I'll be waiting."

My throat feels tight and dry as I head toward my sixth-period class. My pulse is racing, and yet I feel tired. I feel like this a lot lately. I'm sure it must be from the pills—I can tell they are affecting my general health. It's weird because I used to consider myself something of a health freak. Now I'm just a freak. I keep telling myself it's just a matter of time until I quit them altogether. One way or another. But I wonder if I'm just fooling myself all over again. I also wonder how smart it is to take my "afternoon" pill just before I truck on down to City Hall. I wonder if cops are trained to look at your pupils and determine whether or not you're high. And I don't particularly like the idea of being caught in the police station with a pill in my pocket, like they're going to frisk me down. So between classes, I stop by the girls' rest room. The pill reminds me of the sun setting as it swirls round and round in the sink and then finally goes down. I hope I'm not sorry.

I feel like a slug as I walk toward town. I hope I don't fall asleep in the chair while the detective is interrogating me. I still remember how it felt to wake up on that table with them scrutinizing me like I was a germ specimen or something that had fallen from outer space. I can't imagine what Detective Sanders has to ask me about now. Maybe this is all just a setup. Maybe they've finally gotten enough evidence and have decided to charge me with Sammy's murder, but they don't want to make a big scene at school. Of course, this is ridiculous. Why would they care if they made a big scene? But that's how my mind works these days. Paranoia is setting in.

Finally, I am sitting before her. Same chair, same desk, same everything. And as usual it feels too familiar. I don't belong here. Cordial greetings pass between us, as if this is a social occasion, and then she begins.

"I want you to try *really* hard to remember what persons you saw actually talking with Samuel that night, Miranda. I've got a copy of the list you gave me, and I want you to put a check by the name of each person that you feel certain had some sort of a conversation with the deceased."

The deceased? Crud, why can't she just call him Sammy? My eyes feel blurry, like I've got some kind of hazy fog hanging over me, as I try to read the names. I blink several times and then rub my eyes, but it doesn't seem to help. Do I need glasses? Has my drug use ruined my vision?

"Are you okay?"

I sigh. "Just tired, I guess."

"Are you sleeping any better now?"

"Not really." I actually try to look pitiful. "Look, Detective, do you think I could take the list home and really give this some thought? It's been a long day, and I forgot to eat lunch and—"

"Oh, sure, you go ahead. It's just a copy. But I need you to drop it by first thing in the morning. Okay?"

"Yeah. Thanks. I think I'll do a better job this way."

"Good. We want your best effort, Miranda. We've got some possible leads."

"Right."

Somehow I make it home. All I can think is that I *need* an orange pill. I will die if I don't take an orange pill. But I am barely through the door when the phone van drives up and the phone guy has to come in and hook something up. I wait impatiently. Then Samuel starts mewing his head off, and I know he must be hungry since he's gone longer than usual between feedings. I gently remove him from my pocket and place him in the basket that I'm using for his bed now. I've lined it with an old fur muff of Nana's. I think it's rabbit. I doubt that she'll mind since she's pretty much back in her old state of memory loss these days. Anyway, Samuel really seems to like it. He kneads the white fur with his paws like he thinks it's his mother.

I put his milk in the microwave and play with him during the few seconds that it takes for the bell to ding. I'm using a doll-sized baby bottle to feed him with now. Mr. Campton found a couple of these at the drugstore. The phone guy stops to check out Samuel as he's drinking. I have to admit Samuel's pretty cute.

"You ought to take his picture," says the phone guy. "Man, that is one tiny kitten. It's amazing it can survive away from its mother."

"Uh-huh." I continue to feed him without looking up.

"Well, you're all set with your phone now."

"Thanks." But my attention is still on Samuel. The phone guy's comment makes me feel worried. I remind myself that Mr. Campton keeps telling me he's going to do just fine. But then again Mr. Campton is pretty optimistic about a lot of things. I told him about Andi Pierce and how she's moving in this weekend, and I'm pretty sure he'll like her. They seem a bit alike.

Samuel finally falls asleep with milk still dripping off his whiskers. I rinse out the bottle and put it away, then pick up the list from the detective. For the second time I try to study it. It's funny how these names don't seem familiar anymore. It's like they're people I *used* to know. Or thought I knew. But now they seem like complete strangers to me. I force myself to try to remember that night again, but it all seems so long ago now. I feel my eyelids getting heavy and I want to set the list aside, but I remind myself that I promised to turn it in by morning.

I fix myself a bowl of tomato soup and sit down to the list again. It feels like I'm taking a math test or SATs, but my brain just doesn't want to function. Finally I check off the names of a few girls that Sammy danced with as well as a couple of guys he talked to, or at least I think he talked to. I know it's not complete, but it's the best I can do right now. Besides, I have real homework to do.

It occurs to me once again, as I shove the list aside, that Mitch's name is still absent from my list. I know this is totally stupid because I'm positive that other kids have been questioned about that night. And some, like Kyra, have certainly mentioned his presence. Why am I still holding back? So I decide to write his name at the bottom. And then I put a check by his name. I'm not even sure why I do this. It's not spite. It's not really anything. It simply seems like the right thing to do. Anyway, I no longer care about Mitch, and I'm certain he doesn't care about me. We don't even speak in passing. But this is fine with me. That's a slice of my life that I'd just as soon forget. Sometimes when I'm beating myself up over Sammy it occurs to me that I might've paid more attention to Sammy that night if it hadn't been for Mitch. Not that it's Mitch's fault that Sammy died. But he was a distraction.

Now I put the list away. I pull out my economics book and attempt to study for tomorrow's test. At

least tomorrow is Friday—the end of week two.
But after about 20 minutes of hopeless "studying,"
I realize I cannot keep my eyes open. I lean my
head against the sofa, for just a few minutes, I
think. And then, for the first time since I started
taking those stupid pills I actually fall asleep without the aid of one . . . and sleep until morning.

When I wake up, I feel absolutely rotten. My mouth
feels like a dead horse slept there and my head is
throbbing. This is nothing new. I feed Samuel
because he is mewing desperately for food, and as
soon as I'm done, I head straight for Nana's bedroom.

I jerk open the drawer that sticks and retrieve
my two orange pills for the day. But then I decide
I should probably take a third one along, just in
case. So I put those two pills in my pocket and get
out another one. I lift this one to my lips—ready
for some relief. Then I stop and just stare at it.
Why am I doing this? Now, this is the first time I've
ever really questioned my behavior. And it seems
kind of strange.

Always before I've told myself these pills were a
temporary measure—to help me get by until I finish
this thing off for good. Suddenly I wonder why I
continue to take these stupid pills that only make
me feel worse. Oh, sure, they seem to help during the
first hour or two, but then they wear off. I started
out with one of each a day, but now I'm moving up
to three?

I ask myself, what does it matter? Who really

gives a rip? I raise the pill, ready to pop it into my mouth, but I pause again as I notice an object in the open drawer in front of me.

I suppose it's been there all along, but I never really noticed it before. Probably because I'm usually so consumed with consuming my pills. It's nothing so unusual. Just a plain brown velvet-covered box, like from a jewelry counter, not very big or impressive. Probably something that Nana's husband gave her a long time ago. Still, I'm curious. I open the box to see a folded slip of paper lying on top. It's only about three inches square, and my name is written in Nana's shaky handwriting. Her writing used to be quite pretty. When I was in grade school, I would try to imitate it. Then her letters became wobbly and crooked when she started getting Alzheimer's a few years back. Inside the folded paper it says, "For her 16th birthday, now don't forget!" I smile as I remember how she used to leave these little notes everywhere to start out with, before she began to forget everything, including the notes.

Well, it looks as if she forgot this one. I can tell it's a piece of jewelry, some kind of clear pendant on a gold chain. But as I examine it more closely, I can see that it's one of those tiny mustard seeds that are enclosed in a clear glass bead. It's actually kind of pretty—in an old-fashioned sort of way.

Then it hits me—the mustard seed that Andi was trying to explain last weekend. It was the size of faith. Of course I tell myself it's merely a silly coincidence and that mustard-seed necklaces have been around for generations, maybe even centuries. I remove the necklace and fasten it around my neck. If nothing else, it will remind me of Nana—that she once loved me and still loves me, when she can remember such things. But then I remember the time we planted our garden. I remember how Nana said a mustard seed of faith could move a mountain. I didn't get it then, and I'm not sure I get it now, but I think maybe it's worth a try.

I study the tiny pill in my hand. Not much bigger than a mustard seed, but it feels like a mountain to me. Okay, maybe it's just a small hill. It's still something I can't quite seem to get over. Then I look at the white bag, and that seems more like a *real* mountain. I imagine taking a mountain of these pills during the course of my lifetime—if I decide to live, that is. Or taking a small hill of the white pills in one day, if I decide to die. Either way I look at it, it's a mountain.

I reach for the mustard seed in my necklace and wonder. For the first time since childhood Sunday school and blessings at mealtime with Nana, I decide to give this prayer thing a try.

"Okay, God, you want to help me to move this mountain?" I hold the white bag up, as if I'm challenging him. "Be my guest." I stand there for what feels like a couple minutes, not really thinking anything. Just waiting for something—like maybe the sky to fall. Then I begin to cry. For the first time since I started taking these stupid pills, I realize this isn't how I want to live. I don't want to be an addict.

And then, without fully considering what I'm

doing, I impulsively walk into the bathroom. As if in a trance, although I'm fully aware, I open up the two bags and dump the contents into the toilet. I stare at the orange and white dots—they look like happy pieces of party confetti. Then I push the flush handle down. Just like that! I watch in stunned shock as they swirl in a circle, chasing each other down the drain until they are gone. Then I fall on my knees and stare at the clear water in the toilet, suddenly wishing for them back. Oh, what have I done?

With shaking hands, I slip Samuel into my sweat-shirt pocket and head for the police station to drop off my list. Already my head is starting to throb like someone's got a miniature jackhammer going in there. And I am craving, desperately longing for, some kind of chemical help—something to get me through this day. What have I done? Or was it really God? I can't even figure it out.

I drop off my list at the receptionist's desk, then head to school, reminding myself about how much money I spent—wasted—on the very pills that I just flushed down the toilet. What in the world have I done? I must be mad.

As I walk home from school, I'm certain that I failed my economics test, but at least this day is over. I feel shaky and sick and scared, and yet I can't deny that I prayed for God to remove that mountain, and somehow he did. Yes, I know it was my very own hand that dumped the pills and flushed the toilet. But perhaps that's what makes this so amazing. I mean, *why* did I do that? I never meant to do that.

Or did I? In a weird and confusing way, it almost seems like a miracle. Even if it seems like a bad one just now.

And so as I walk toward home, I pray for the second time in one day. This time I actually ask God to help me. I beg him to show me some way out of this trap that has become my so-called life.

"I want that clean slate," I pray with tears now rolling down my cheeks. "I want that fresh start." Fortunately, no one is around to see me babbling like this. Not that I really care anymore. Because the truth is, I don't. In fact, I'm so desperate that I think I could scream it out for the whole neighborhood—the whole world—to hear. Local Girl Is Looking for God!

Later in the afternoon, after we've both had our after-school snack, I take Samuel out with me to the backyard. I've decided we need to make a memorial for his departed family. I find Nana's old garden shovel and dig a hole next to the bed of daylilies. They look so cheerful with their golden faces looking toward the sky. Then I gently remove what remains of Samuel's siblings, trying not to look too closely as I place them in a tissue-lined tin that I found in Nana's pantry. It has holly and berries on it and once contained Christmas cookies, but I think it'll do. I set this in the hole and start to cover it with damp soil.

"What're you doing there, Miranda?"

I turn to see Mr. Campton walking toward me.

"Burying the other kittens." I wonder if he'll think I'm silly, but he just smiles.

"Well, good for you. I'd thought about doing that myself, but hadn't gotten around to it."

"It just seemed like the right thing to do."

Then his eyes light up. "You wait right here and I'll be back." He shuffles away as I refill and then smooth the dirt on top of the grave.

When he returns he has something in his hand. "How about if we use this to mark their grave?" He holds up a roughly made wooden cross.

"Did you make that?"

He smiles sheepishly. "Well, I'd planned to go out and fetch that mother cat and give her a fitting burial. But by the time I got this cross finished and found an old shoe box, somebody else, maybe the city, already picked her up." He sighs. "But I'd be glad to use it for her babies. She was a good old cat, even if she was a little on the wild side."

I sigh too. "She may not have really wanted to be wild. Maybe she just didn't have the right kind of upbringing, you know."

"You're probably right about that, Miranda." Slowly he stoops down and pushes the cross into the soil. "How's that?"

I turn and smile, actually smile, at him. "That's perfect."

Then we both stand there for a quiet moment, and I think maybe we're both praying. I don't actually form any real words in my mind, but it's like I'm breathing them out somehow. For the first time in a long time—maybe forever—a sensation of what feels like peace comes over me. It's hard to explain—kind of like a sigh, or the way I feel when I finish a race. Whatever it is, it feels like a beginning.

Then we sit down for a while and just visit. I show him how Samuel is doing, how much he has grown. I tell him about the bed I made and how Samuel can easily empty a whole bottle at one feeding now. Of course, the bottles aren't very big, but then neither is Samuel. Finally, it's getting late, and Mr. Campton decides he better go inside.

"This cool damp air plays havoc with my rheumatism," he says as he pushes himself up from the chair.

"It'll be nice when summer comes." I stand too.

"I 'spect you have some big plans for your evening . . . being it's a Friday and all."

"Not really."

He brightens now. "Well, I'm not much of a cook, but I've got me a pot of stew warming in there. I made a mess of it yesterday, and it's always better the second time around."

"That sounds good."

He smiles. "Well, come on in."

And so I sit with Mr. Campton at his little plastic-topped table, the kind that was popular in the '50s, and we eat stew and saltine crackers together. I think it's one of the best meals I've ever eaten. I insist on cleaning up, and he never stops talking while I take my time washing all the dishes—it looks like two days' worth, but I don't mind.

Afterwards he shows me photos of his wife, children, and grandchildren, as well as Bill Junior's army photo and Purple Heart medal—these hold the place of honor right in the center of the old carved oak mantel. Finally, I can tell he's getting tired, so I make an excuse to leave.

"It was right nice sharing a meal with you, Miranda," he says, smiling.

"Thank you, Mr. Campton. I really enjoyed it. Next time you'll have to let me cook."

He grins. "Your nana used to say the same thing."

And so I'm thinking maybe this can be a regular thing as I walk back to my apartment. Then I notice my apartment door doesn't seem to be completely closed. At first I think of Shelby, but earlier I'd thought I heard her car leaving. I glance out to the street to be sure, then see Hale Ramsey's Camaro. I feel a white rage coming on.

I go into Nana's apartment to find Hale and Tyrone sitting in the living room. There's a new six-pack on the cracked coffee table, as well as a grocery bag full of who knows what else. They're both just sitting there like they own the place.

"What do you guys think you're doing?" I demand, remaining by the front door. I'm leaving it open just in case.

"Hey, Miranda." Tyrone stands and smiles. "We didn't mean to bust in here, but we knocked and no one answered, and your door was open, so we just figured we'd wait until you got back."

"Howdy, Mirandy!" Hale grins and holds up a beer bottle. "Come and join the party."

Despite my fury, I decide to use my head for a change as I consider my options. First of all, I have no intention of joining the party. But on the other hand, I don't really want to make them mad at me. For all I know they could be vindictive, and it's not like I have anyone to come to my defense these days. Even though Mr. Campton would, I know his hearing is poor and he's not exactly in his prime. Anyway, I realize it would be best to get them to leave peacefully. But I'm not sure how to do this. I can feel Samuel in my pocket and, for some reason, I don't want these guys to see my kitten. I realize that's stupid and slightly paranoid, but I make my excuse anyway.

"I've got to go do something. I'll be right back." Then I slip into the bedroom and safely tuck Samuel in a sweater-lined drawer. *This ought to keep him out of harm's way,* I think. Not that I expect trouble, really. You just never know.

Then I come out and, placing my hands on my hips, I force a smile as I say, "Look, you guys. I'm not really into this—"

"Come on, Miranda," urges Tyrone. "You used to be such a party girl."

"Yeah, we're just trying to be social." Hale lifts up the six-pack. "Have a brewski and see if that don't just taste like you put your foot in it."

"Huh?"

Tyrone rolls his eyes. It must be his trademark around Hale. "Never mind him, Miranda. Come on and sit down. Honest, girl, we just wanted to stop by and see how you're doing. You go slipping around the halls at school like some kinda ghost girl. I never see you talking to anyone anymore. You need friends." He smiles. "And we're here to help."

Despite myself, I think Tyrone seems sincere. And maybe he is. But still, I want them to leave. I'd rather be alone. "I appreciate that, Tyrone." I sigh. "And I know I've been pretty down. But I'm doing better now."

"Those pills perk you right up, did they?" Hale eyes me curiously.

I shrug and look away.

"How're they working for you?" Hale continues, as if he's some kind of doctor. "You sure you got enough to get you through a whole month? Sometimes they start to wear down after a while and you need to up the dose. There are other things you can use too—"

"Actually," I say, cutting him off, "I've decided not to use them anymore."

Hale's brows lift. "Serious?"

"Yeah. I'm done with that."

"Just like that?" Hale seems really puzzled. "What makes you so sure?"

I consider this. "Do you really want to know?"

"Of course."

"Well, I've been thinking about God lately. I know it sounds weird. But one day I was about to take another pill and I asked God to help me not to." I can see the skepticism in their eyes. But I go on anyway. "And he did."

Tyrone's eyes seem to be questioning. "So what did God do?"

"He helped me to flush them down the toilet," I say firmly.

"You what?" Hale leans forward with huge eyes.

"You're pulling my tail now, ain't you, Mirandy? You paid good money for that stuff. Nobody flushes that kind of money down the can like that."

Tyrone is strangely silent.

So Hale goes on. "You could've sold them. Are you crazy?"

"What's it to you?" I fire back. "They were my pills, my money."

"You could've given them back to me," Hale continues. "I would've sold them."

"Look, I just didn't like the feeling of having to take them all the time just to make it through another day—or to sleep at night. And I didn't like how they made me feel—or needing to use more. It's like I wasn't even alive when I was using that stuff." I sit down in the rocker as the realization hits me. "And I suppose I didn't *want* to be alive. But *now* I do."

Hale frowns like he's just lost his best friend.

Tyrone's head is down. I have to admit I feel sorry for him just now. His brown hair is drooping over his eyes as he's hunched over like that—so dejected looking. Then I notice the tag sticking out from the back of his shirt. As I look closer, I realize it's because his shirt is on inside out.

"Hey, Ty," I say, hoping to lighten up the subject, "did you know your shirt's on inside out?"

He looks up at me, but his eyes look flat and dull. "Yeah, I know."

"Oh." I wonder if he's using himself—and, if so, what he's on right now . . . besides the beer, that is.

Hale chuckles. "He does that on purpose some-times."

"So what?" Tyrone straightens up, takes a swig of beer, and suddenly leans back.

"Why?" I ask. But even as I ask I'm thinking about something entirely different. I'm remembering the night of my party. And that nondescript brown-haired guy, with his back to me, talking to Sammy. His head bent toward Sammy as if he was telling him a joke or giving him something. And there was a tag sticking out from his dark-colored shirt. I don't know why I remember that detail, but it's as plain as day.

Tyrone now looks defiant, as if he's exasperated with the world in general. "Well, I'll tell you. I refuse to conform to capitalist dictations for the clothing industry."

"Huh?" I manage to say.

"Okay, it's like this—when Nike pays me to wear a Nike shirt, *then* I'll advertise for them."

"I still don't get—"

"Look, my stepmother still buys me Nike T-shirts sometimes. Because she doesn't get it. So rather than be a walking billboard for some megacompany that uses third-world slave labor, I just turn the T-shirt inside out. Get it?"

I nod.

Hale chuckles. "Sorry you asked?"

"No, actually I'm glad I asked." I smile at Tyrone. "I can respect that." Suddenly it seems perfectly clear what I must do. It's time for my best perfor-mance yet.

"Really?" Tyrone looks up curiously.

"Yeah." I glance down at the beers. "You and Hale still offering?"

They nod.

"Sure," Tyrone says. "Help yourself."

I open the bottle and hold it up as if to make a toast. "Here's to friends."

Hale and Tyrone follow my lead.

"Hey, we got some chips." Tyrone reaches for the grocery bag.

"Cool. I'll get a bowl." I can feel my hands shaking as I go to the kitchen for a bowl. It's not that I'm scared exactly, just nervous. I don't want to blow this. I pause at the sink and pour out about half of my beer, then return with a salad bowl.

"All right." Hale slaps his knees as I dump the bag of chips into the bowl and set it in the center of the table. "Now this smells more like a real *partee.*"

I grab a handful of chips. "Just because I don't want to do the pills anymore doesn't mean I don't want to have some fun."

"Yeah," Tyrone puts in, "there's lots of ways to have fun."

So we sit and visit and joke, and before long another six-pack is pulled out of the bag. Cheaper beer now, in the can. Somehow I manage to pour most of my beer, except for a few tiny sips, down the sink, and these guys think I'm still Miranda the party girl.

I put some music on and return to the kitchen to throw away some empty cans and pour some more beer down the drain. Hale surprises me by joining me in there.

"Let's boogie, Mirandy," he says with a big grin.

"Nah, I don't really feel like it." I lean against the counter and study him. He's frowning now, probably thinking I'm a great big waste of time. Suddenly I wonder what I could've been thinking. What if I'm making a huge mistake here? What made me think I could catch them in this silly little game where they make the rules?

"You just need to loosen up more," says Hale. "You should have another brewski."

"Nah, I think I've had enough beer. This was fun, but maybe it's time to call it a night."

He frowns again. "Aw, come on, Mirandy, you were just starting to have fun."

I attempt to look something between confused and frustrated. "Yeah, but it's still hard, you know. I mean, after what happened to Sammy, well, it's like I can't really loosen up and have fun anymore."

And then Hale gets this little smile. "Hang on a minute."

I act like I'm interested. And I hold my breath as he walks out of the kitchen. I can hear him rustling in the paper bag again. Then he returns with a big smile and something tucked in his hand.

"I've got just what you need, little lady."

I smile and look down into his open palm to see a round yellow disk with what looks like a smiley face on it. "Cute," I say. "Looks like candy."

"Way better than candy." He holds it out.

I decide to play dumb now. "But what is it?"

"Something to help you relax and loosen up. Trust me. You'll like it."

"Is it safe?"

"Sure, when you know what you're doing. And I know what I'm doing."

Now I'm feeling a mixture of excitement laced with fear. I've gotten all the information I need from them. But what do I do next? Take the pill and pretend to swallow it? Or refuse and risk offending these guys? I feel like I've baited the wolves and now they're sitting in my living room. How do I get them out?

Once again I decide to pray for help. "Just a minute," I say as I turn away from Hale and face the sink, stalling as I get myself a glass of water. And suddenly it hits me. I know just what to do. I lean over the sink and clutch my stomach and groan as if I'm going to puke. "Oh, no," I groan, hoping my face looks sick.

Then I make this mad dash for the bathroom, lock the door, and proceed to make what I think are very realistic hurling sounds. I go on like this for several minutes, flushing the toilet occasionally for special sound effects. Then I run water in the sink as if I'm washing my face. I even slap my cheeks to make them look sort of blotchy and then finally I come back out, still holding my stomach with a face that might possibly win an Oscar.

"Sorry, guys," I say in this peevish voice. "I think I'm really sick. I don't know if it was the beer or what. But I—"

And then I make another sprint for the bathroom.

This time I stay in there for a long time. I make barfing sounds and groan. Once again, I run water and flush the toilet. Finally I go and listen at the door, curious as to whether they're still here or not. It occurs to me that my act might be too convincing, that they may be worried about me and stick around to make sure I'm okay. Friends would do that.

But when I finally crack open the door and peer out, they are gone. All that's left is their last empties and a few broken chips at the bottom of the bowl. I lock the front door and go to check on Samuel. Naturally, he is ready to eat. My hands tremble as I try to pour milk into the small opening of the bottle. I cannot believe what I have just done. I don't really know what difference it will make in the end, or if it will get me into trouble with these guys. But I know what I have to do now, and I fully intend to do it.

I realize that Detective Sanders probably won't be at her desk tonight, but I decide to call anyway. I know that she has voice mail. After a brief period of canned Muzak, I get through to her automated message and I begin to speak. "This is Miranda Sanchez, and I have just discovered something that might be helpful in the case. Call me if you want to talk about it." Then I hang up and glance over my shoulder, as if I'm afraid that Hale or Tyrone might still be lurking in the apartment and fully aware of what I'm up to. I feel slightly paranoid as I check behind the sofa and the curtains. But I suspect this could be a dangerous game that I'm playing. And I know this makes me a narc now. But I don't care. I'm doing it for Sammy.

It's Saturday and Andi is moving in today. I introduce her to Mr. Campton and help carry boxes and small pieces of furniture upstairs. Fortunately she doesn't have much.

"I've been trying to go minimalist," she explains as we set her futon in the corner. "It's easier that way when you're still in college and moving around a lot. But one of these days I'm going to buy a real dining table. I think I'll go for a long narrow one, like they have in Italy, and then you line all your friends up and have a great big dinner that goes on until late at night."

"Have you been to Italy?" I venture.

"Yeah. Some friends and I went before our senior

year of college. It was so awesome. I want to go again."

"Cool." I move toward the door.

"Thanks for the help." She stands now and reties the bandana that's been keeping her hair back. "You doing okay?"

I actually smile. "As a matter of fact, I am."

"Wanna tell me about it later?" she asks as she opens up a box.

"Yeah. Maybe when you're more settled in."

"Cool."

I think about Andi and her long table as I walk downstairs. For some reason that appeals to me too. I wish I had a table like that. And friends to line it with. I remember the list of names I made for Detective Sanders—the kids who were at my party that night. I realize how few of them were real friends. But I must still have a few friends. I decide to make a new list. Even if I can only think of two people, it will be a start.

1. Mr. Campton—okay, he's old but nice.
2. Andi Pierce—not so old, but someone I think I can depend on.
3. Jamie Cantrell—my age and very loyal.
4. Dylan Gray—haven't talked for a while, but I feel he can be trusted.
5. Bethany Gray—a child maybe, but the spirit of an angel.
6. Taylor Wilson—good athlete and dependable friend.
7. Rebecca Landis—possibilities.

Then for good measure I add,

1. Nana—whether or not she's in her right mind.
2. Shelby—maybe someday, when we both
   grow up.

I figure I can use the friends-and-family plan.
It helps to pad the list a little. Two names are conspicuously absent. Both end with James. I try not
to think about this.

I've decided it's time to do laundry since most
of my clothes are smelly and dirty. I was forced to
pull out my old overalls—the ones that Kyra made
me promise last fall to never wear again. She said
they make me look like a cow and actually suggested that I burn them. But I simply buried them
in the back of my closet. Now I'm wearing them,
and I don't think they look half bad, if I do say so
myself. Besides, farming runs in my family.

I'm carrying a clean basket of whites when I
hear a knock on the door. First I jump, thinking
it might be Hale and Tyrone, stopping by to party
again. But my door is securely locked, and I have
no intention of letting them in. I peer through the
peephole and drop the basket when I see who's
standing out there.

It's Kyra. A deep frown is carved into her face.
I can't even imagine why she's here. I actually look
down at her hand, thinking she might possibly have
a gun. But I see a white sheet of paper there instead.
I unlock the door and open it.

"Hi," I begin. "Do you want to come—?"

But she just shoves the paper at me. "Here. I thought you should have this."

I take the paper and she turns away. And just like that she climbs into her car and drives off, fast. I hold the paper up to see, but my hand is shaking so badly that I cannot even read it. I'm afraid it's legal papers—like a warrant or a summons. Perhaps I am being charged with criminal misconduct or murder or something. But why would *she* deliver it? I close and lock the door and, kicking the laundry basket aside, make my way to the table. I lay the page on the table, take a deep breath, and sit down. I force my eyes to focus and discover this paper isn't typed or even legal looking. It's handwritten, and has been photocopied, possibly out of some sort of notebook or journal. But the writing is painfully familiar. Chunky, square, and masculine. I've been able to recognize Sammy's handwriting since childhood. This appears to be a poem.

M.S. the Tenderhearted

Remember the dead mouse
And how you cried
You insisted we bury it.
Then I broke my arm
You gave me "Biff the Bear"
Until I felt better.
Then your dad left
And you couldn't smile
But I was your clown
And you smiled for me

So I would feel better.
Your heart is so tender, M.S.
It's like a rose petal
I would like to wrap
Myself in it and rest.
I pray it never breaks
Never changes.
And if it belonged to me
I would cherish it always
For you will always be
M.S. the Tenderhearted.

S.J.

I am crying so hard now that I must move the paper away before I soak it and ruin it with my tears. I'd forgotten how Sammy used to call me that sometimes. "Miranda Sanchez the Tenderhearted." Like it was some sort of title he'd bestowed upon me. I used to act as if I didn't like it, especially as we got older. When we were about 14 and Kyra and I were watching a sad video at the Jameses', Sammy caught me crying. He elbowed me and said, "Hey, M.S. the Tenderhearted strikes again." At first I felt hurt and slightly betrayed. I thought he was teasing me. But then I saw his eyes. I realized it was just his way of saying, "It's okay. Don't feel bad for crying." It was our secret code. But I'd almost forgotten it.

I'm not sure if Kyra brought this poem to me as a form of torture, or perhaps something else. But as I sob into what *was* a clean pillowcase I don't feel that these are such bad tears after all. I wonder if there's such a thing as *healing* tears. And if there is, I think this may be what's happening.

Then I get up and add Kyra James' name to my friends-and-family list. She is number 10, and my comment next to her name is, "This might take a miracle. But I'm starting to believe that maybe miracles do happen."

I reread the poem and then start crying all over again. I'm sure if Sammy were here he'd call me "M.S. the Tenderhearted," but then that would be okay. I just wish he were here right now. *Oh, Sammy, where are you?*

The sound of knocking startles me and I jump up, expecting to see Hale and Tyrone or perhaps Kyra again. Will she demand the poem back? But it's Andi this time. I open the door, and she eyes me curiously.

"Been crying?"

I nod. "Wanna come in?"

"Yeah. I thought maybe I could borrow a can opener. I know I have one, but I can't find it any-where. I was going to warm up some soup." She looks around the apartment and smiles. "This is cute."

"You mean an old-lady kind of cute?"

"Yeah. But it's cozy and charming too."

"And if you need to borrow anything—" I wave my hand toward the cluttered kitchen—"it's probably here."

"Looks like it."

"So why are you crying?" she asks as she sits down on the sofa amidst my socks and underwear.

I retrieve the can opener and hand it to her. "I was just reading this poem that Sammy wrote."

"For you?"

"Yeah. Kyra dropped it by."

Her brows lift as if she's slightly surprised. "Well, good for her."

"Yeah. Kind of unexpected."

"Well, people can change."

"Yeah, I guess." I wish that were true.

"So Sammy wrote you a poem. That's pretty special."

"Yeah. I cried both times I read it."

"He must've really liked you, Miranda."

I feel myself choking up again. "Yeah."

"You guys weren't exactly going out or anything though, were you?"

I shake my head. "We've always been really good friends, you know, like brother and sister. I kind of grew up with Kyra and Sammy. But I was really closer to Sammy—or I used to be."

"But he wrote you a poem?"

I nod.

"Do you think he was in love with you?"

I nod again.

"Were you in love with him?"

Now I really start to cry. I sit down in the recliner and bury my face in my hands and just sob. "I don't know. I loved him—I know I loved him. I guess I thought, you know, maybe someday—"

I feel her standing beside me now. Her hand is rubbing my back. And she's telling me it's going to be okay. But I'm not sure how she can know this.

I mean, I felt like things were getting better. But now this. Finally I look up and say, "I just—I just—I want to know where he is right now. I want to know he's . . . all right."

She sits back down and waits for me to calm down. I wipe my nose on a sweat sock and draw in a long jagged breath. "I just want to know."

"I can understand that. All I can tell you is that Sammy was a believer. His relationship with God was real. And so I believe he's in heaven right now. Probably having the time of his life."

"Really? You really believe that?"

"I do."

Then I tell her about my mustard seed and my prayers, and suddenly she starts laughing and smiling like that's the best news she's heard in years. "Oh, Miranda, that is so cool. Do you know how happy that must make Sammy feel?"

"Huh?"

"I have a feeling that folks in heaven are aware of some of the things that go on down here on earth."

We talk some more and finally Andi invites me up to her place for some chicken-noodle soup, and I accept. And although we're only sitting at a small card table, she lights a purple candle, and somehow it feels like a feast to me. When she bows her head to bless the food, she says, "Hey, God, thanks for the soup and my friend Miranda here. You are so awesome! By the way, give our regards to Sammy—I'm sure he's having one whopping party right now, knowing that his good buddy Miranda is going to be just fine."

I wake up to the phone ringing at around 7:30 Monday morning. I leap from bed and trip over my jogging shoes trying to grab it. "Hello?"

"Miranda?"

"Uh-huh."

"This is Detective Sanders. I got your message. What's up?"

So I launch into the whole story about Hale and Tyrone. "I don't know if this is helpful or not," I finally say. "And it's not like I want to get them in trouble, but I just don't want what happened to Sammy to happen to anyone else. You know?"

"Yes. I know. Are you willing to make a statement?"

I consider this. "Do they have to know that I'm the one who told?"

"I'll see what we can do. I can understand your concerns."

Then I remember how those two guys left me alone when I was in the bathroom pretending to be sick. What if I'd taken their tablet and gotten sick for real? "Yeah," I say with conviction, "I'll make a statement."

And so I go in, missing my first class, and make my statement. It only takes about 30 minutes. "Do you think this is it?" I ask the detective. "Will I have to come back?"

"You might have to testify. Are you okay with that?"

"Yeah . . . ," I say slowly. "I guess so. I can do it for Sammy."

She smiles. "Thanks."

As I walk to school I experience a gnawing in the pit of my stomach. Real fear. What will Hale and Tyrone do if they find out? Have I put myself in unnecessary danger? Finally, I realize that the only thing I can do is pray. And I pray all the way to school. I find this oddly calming.

It's just after fourth period when I notice a thick cluster of kids around the hallway next to the office. Normally I would avoid this sort of situation—after losing Sammy, that is. But today I decide to go take a look. I get there just in time to see a uniformed officer taking Tyrone away. But Hale is nowhere to be seen. I'm not surprised since I haven't seen him in any classes today. I wonder if he's already been picked up. Or maybe he's on the run. I feel fairly certain that Tyrone's unexpected trip to the police station is a result of my statement. And I guess this troubles me a bit.

It's weird because I actually thought I'd feel some relief right now. But I mostly feel sad. I don't really know those two guys that well, but I have a feeling there's a whole lot more to their stories. I have a feeling that there are other factors in play here. I know how I felt when it seemed like I was the only one to blame for Sammy's death. And believe me, I know that I am *partially* to blame. There's no escaping that. But I think I've come to understand that there are degrees of guilt. And like Andi once said, "We're all a little bit guilty."

As the crowd starts to break apart, joking and speculating over the possible reasons that Tyrone has been picked up by the cops, I reach up and clutch my mustard-seed pendant. And right there in Macon High's main hallway, I pray a silent prayer for all of us. I ask God to have mercy on us and to see us through this thing.

Epilogue

The day has finally come. Only two months since that horrible night when Sammy died, and we are here today to be questioned by the court. I thought I'd feel a lot sadder right now. But mostly I'm just nervous. And scared. Of course, the sadness is still here, and it's amplified when I see Kyra and her family coming into the courthouse. I avert my gaze and pretend to be preoccupied with the bulletin board beside me. Not so much because I don't want to see them, but because I don't think they want to see me. I'm sure that I make them uncomfortable.

Kyra keeps her eyes straight forward as she walks past me toward the waiting area. She sits down next to the assistant D.A., a serious-looking woman who never seems to smile. Not that this is a time for smiling. Kyra's parents sit next to her, subdued and expressionless, but wearing their grief like a gray gauzy tent that shrouds their whole family in sorrow. Suddenly I wonder if we'll ever get over this. Any of us.

I've given up the hope of my life ever returning to normal. In fact, I'm convinced that normal doesn't exist. I'm settling for survival at the moment. I've adopted the old AA oath of living one day at a time—actually, I think it was Jesus who first said it. Anyway, I believe it's the only way to endure something like this. I don't know what the outcome of this day will be. Detective Sanders has made it clear that, despite my help, they can make no promises one way or another. No one will know what's to be until we hear everyone's testimony and the court makes its decision. And although I've been assured it's not likely, I'm prepared to go to jail. It could happen.

And I must admit that the thought of doing time doesn't bother me nearly as much as it did two months ago. Because now I believe that God will see me through this—no matter what comes. And that makes all the difference.

Do I wish I could turn back the calendar and change what happened in March? Of course! I would do anything to have Sammy back. But I realize what's done is done, and we the survivors must continue to move forward. We must take our various consequences and accept our own responsibility for all our individual degrees of guilt. I am ready.

degrees OF GUILT

Sammy's dead. . .they each played a part.
Kyra, his twin sister. Miranda, the girl
he loved. And Tyrone, a friend from school.

WHAT'S THE REAL STORY?

There's always more than one point
of view—read all three.

kyra's story
DANDI DALEY MACKALL

miranda's story
MELODY CARLSON

tyrone's story
SIGMUND BROUWER

For insider info and surprising revelations, go to
www.degreesofguilt.com.
Enter code guilt02,
and you'll be able to watch Miranda's video interview
and read her court transcript too.

A Sneak Peek at Kyra's Story . . .

The phone rings as soon as we step into the house.
Mom picks it up. "Hello?"

I'm on the second step, heading upstairs, but I
can tell by Mom's phone voice it's a guy, probably
for me. She covers the receiver with her palm.
"Kyra, for you!"

"Who is it?" I ask.

"P.J. Something?"

She means D.J., and I don't feel like rehashing
Vin Diesel's career. I don't know if I want to go out
with D.J. again or not. "Tell him I'm not here!"
I call down.

Mom hollers, "Kyra?" She's against lies of the
bald-faced variety.

"Tell him I have a headache." It's the excuse
I gave Dad in the restaurant when he wanted me

to eat a roll. As soon as I say it, I realize it's true now. I really do have a headache.

I trot on upstairs. Mom will handle D.J. better than I could right now. She never wants to discourage any of them. If she only knew. . . .

I'm not sure what's wrong with me, why I don't feel like talking to D.J. or to anybody, why I don't want to think about school tomorrow, but then I *do* want to think about it.

Sammy's changed into sweats already and is headed back down the stairs, basketball in hand.

I block his path near the top of the stairs. "Sammy, do you still have your econ book from last semester?" I've put off economics as long as possible. Mr. Hatt will be the only teacher I haven't taken before. I want to make a good impression and get that over with. It would help if I could glance through the text before class.

"Yeah, right." Sammy bounces the ball on the stairs and then folds his long arms around it. "My beloved econ book is right beside my bed with my algebra book, framed." He fakes left and twirls past me on the right.

My muscles jerk in the pit of my stomach. I'm so tired of worrying about everything . . . and nothing. I don't want to think anymore, not about econ or school or D.J. or Vin Diesel. Not about anything.

I open the door to my room and wonder why it doesn't feel more like home, like *my* room. I got to choose new wallpaper last year, but I went with the one I could tell Mom was rooting for—

sky blue with slightly raised white puffs through it. It looks fine. I wouldn't have known what else to pick.

The desk is built in like a long counter with drawers on both sides. I never study there though. I sit on the floor or on my bed. The only poster, tack-mounted on my closet door, is the one Miranda gave me during her Beatles phase. John Lennon, looking so sad you could almost believe he knew what was coming.

I don't collect things like most of my friends. So the glass figurines on my wall shelf are things people have given me.

The CD tower by my bed is full, mostly with CDs guys have liked and given me or burned copies for me. When I dated Drew, I pretended to like the rap he ran through his car speakers, so he burned me about 20 rap CDs. Same with Dan, only he was into heavy metal.

I take the bottom CD without looking at it and stick it in my portable player. Then I plop onto my bed and lean back, facing the white, stucco ceiling.

I crank up the volume all the way before I put on the headphones. I like the surprise, the shock of sound when I slip on the headset. It's loud—head-shaking, teeth-jarring loud—like I've stepped inside a tunnel where I can't escape, but neither can the music.

A Sneak Peek at Tyrone's Story . . .

Macon, Iowa, is a small town. The kind of town where farmers actually drive tractors to the post office and the women trade recipes down at the local grocery store. I did not grow up here, of course. I grew up in Chicago, in an area of luxury high-rises that overlooked Lake Michigan.

It wasn't until my freshman year that I arrived in Macon, straight from a private school in Chicago where we all wore identical school uniforms and demerits were issued for shirts, ties, or pants that weren't sufficiently ironed free of any wrinkles. No wonder, huh, that I've decided to wear what I like when I like, even if that means turning shirts inside out to hide the corporate labels.

Any new school is tough to crack. It's tough enough to go from an elite private school to a rowdy public school. But imagine what it's like on the first day when basically all the other students have known each other their entire lives.

Because that was Macon High. Small, filled with classes where all the students had been in the same classes together since their kindergarten years.

It took me six months to find my niche, to stake it out, and to protect it so that at least I was accepted as part of the scenery. Not that I fit in. But I was accepted for not fitting in.

I wasn't alone in feeling like a stranger on that first day. There was one other person new to the school.

Hale Ramsey.

Who would immediately share my misery.

And, I was to find out later, much much more.

About the Author

Melody Carlson is the award-winning author of
more than 90 books for children, teens, and adults—
with sales totaling more than two million. In addi-
tion to *Miranda's Story,* her young adult best-sellers
include the Diary of a Teenage Girl series (Mult-
nomah), which has received great reviews and a
large box of fan mail, as well as *Looking for Cas-
sandra Jane* (Tyndale), *Finding Alice* (Waterbrook),
and the four titles in the Allison Chronicles, a teen
historical series (Bethany House).

Over the years Melody Carlson has worn many
hats—from preschool teacher to youth counselor
to political activist to senior editor. But most of all,
she *loves to write!* Currently she freelances from her
home. Melody and her husband, Chris, who now
have two grown sons, have always had a great heart

for teens—they met twenty-five years ago as Young Life counselors. For a number of years they took troubled teens into their home.

Melody and Chris live in Central Oregon with their chocolate Lab retriever. They enjoy skiing, hiking, gardening, camping, and biking in the beautiful Cascade Mountains.

www.areUthirsty.com
www.degreesofguilt.com